New Beginnings

ANNIE SEATON

Duckinwilla Days: Book 5

Heartwarming and compelling tales of love, self-discovery, and second chances in the heart of rural Australia.

ISBN 978-1-7642184-5-0

The Johnson family

Grandmère and Papa: Margot and Robert Johnson

The parents: Hugo and Ellen Johnson

The Johnson siblings:

Charlotte Johnson - Book 1 - *Coming Home*

Julien Johnson -Book 2 - *Secrets and Surprises*

Oliver Johnson - Book 3 - *Wishes and Whispers*

Guy Johnson - Book 4 - *Chasing Dreams*

Amelia Johnson - Book 5 - *New Beginnings*

Lisette Johnson - Book 6 - *Together at Last*

Chapter 1

Amelia Johnson stood at the sink, scrubbing the saucepans from dinner last night with more force than necessary. Her hair—a striking combination of electric blue, pink and silver that caught the light like a disco ball—was pulled back in a messy bun, and she wore her favourite ripped jeans and an oversized flannel shirt that had seen better days. Her hours at the pre-school had dropped a couple of weeks ago, and now that she had extra time at home, she was feeling more like Cinderella every day.

Reflections from the crystal Mum bought at the markets last week, when she helped Sarah, bathed the farmhouse kitchen in flashes of colour. Mum had headed out early again today, and Amelia suspected it was because she preferred looking after Jett, Sarah's little boy, to being at home.

'I'll be back about three, love. There are a couple of loads of work clothes in the laundry, and upstairs could do with a good vacuum.' Mum had tapped on her door about six-thirty.

'Okay, Mum. I won't be home this

afternoon, though. Say hello to Sarah and Jett for me.'

Amelia didn't mind helping Mum out; it was good to see her getting away from the drudge of looking after four adults, two of whom were really peeing her off lately. Even though Guy and Oli had moved out to live with their respective partners, they still treated the house the same way they always had, expecting Mum to clean up after them.

'You know, there are dishwashers for that sort of thing.' Guy's voice broke into her thoughts.

'What?'

'I said there are dishwashers for that sort of thing,' her brother commented from his seat at the kitchen table, not looking up from his laptop where he was updating his spreadsheets. 'Revolutionary technology, really.'

'And you know there's actual work to be done outside instead of fiddling with spreadsheets all morning,' Amelia shot back, though there was no real heat in her voice. 'Revolutionary concept, really.'

Oliver wandered in through the back door,

his boots leaving small clumps of red dirt on the mat despite Amelia's repeated warnings about cleaning them first. 'What's revolutionary?' he asked, heading straight for the kettle.

'Nothing,' Guy replied at the same time Amelia said, 'Your apparent inability to use a doormat.'

Oliver glanced down at his boots with a surprised expression. 'They're not that bad.'

'They're never that bad in your opinion,' Amelia said, abandoning the pots to grab a tea towel and start drying with the same aggressive energy she'd applied to washing them. 'Yet somehow Mum and I are always sweeping dried clumps of mud out of the kitchen. If we told Sarah what a grub you are when you're here, I'm sure that would be the end of your relationship. Do you wipe your feet at her place?'

'I guess I do. Sorry, I'll use the mat next time.' Oliver switched the kettle on and settled into his usual chair. 'But I have more important things to worry about today.'

'Like what? Whether your precious mangoes are getting enough sunshine?' Amelia rolled her eyes. At twenty-two, she was the youngest of the Johnson siblings, and sometimes she felt like her opinions carried as much weight as one of *Grandmère* 's feather boas.

The sound of slow, uneven footsteps on the stairs interrupted their bickering. Their father appeared in the doorway, fully dressed for farm work but with a confused expression that set Amelia's nerves jangling.

'Morning, Dad,' Oliver said. 'Sleep well?'

Hugo Johnson stood in the kitchen entrance, his callused hands gripping the doorframe as if supporting himself. 'Have you boys turned the pumps off yet?' he asked, his voice carrying that uncertain quality that had become increasingly frequent over the past month or so. It was hard to see her strong dad like this. He'd never fully recovered from his heart attack.

'Yes, Dad,' Guy replied gently, closing his laptop. 'Oliver took care of them at dawn.'

Hugo's brow furrowed as he patted his pockets absently. 'Right. Now, where did I put my work gloves? I could have sworn—'

'They're in your back pocket, Dad,' Amelia said softly, watching as relief flooded her father's face when he found them exactly where she'd said.

'Thank you, sweetheart.' Hugo smiled at her, but his eyes were cloudy. Amelia's chest tightened. 'I don't know where my head is today.'

These moments of confusion seemed to be happening more often—Dad repeated questions, misplaced things, and seemed genuinely confused about routine tasks. But whenever she'd tried to voice her concerns, her siblings had dismissed them as stress or fatigue, but she had noticed the worry on Mum's face more often this week.

Dad headed out to the shed, and Guy looked up from his laptop. 'Everything all right, Melie?'

'Don't call me that. I'm not a kid anymore. And yes, everything's just peachy. Why wouldn't it be? Just because I'm stuck here helping Mum half the week, washing dishes and sweeping up after you two while you sit around planning the future of the farm without consulting the one person who still lives here full-time—'

'Hang on,' Oliver interrupted, staring at her. 'What do you mean, we don't consult you? What do you want to be consulted about? I thought you were moving out anyway.'

'What do you think, Oli? When's the last time anyone asked my opinion about anything important around here?' Amelia demanded, waving the tea towel. 'Charlotte gets to make all the decisions about *Maison de Rêve*. Julien runs the General Store; you control the mangoes. Lisette left to find her own life. Guy and Dad manage the cane and the books—and what do I get a say in? Working part-time at the preschool and helping Mum do the dishes and laundry, with the family assuming I'm too young to understand anything about farming.'

The gentle humming of the refrigerator was the only sound in the ensuing silence.

'That's not fair,' Guy said quietly. 'Of course we value your input. If you want more, just say.'

'Do you?' Amelia challenged. 'Because last week, when I suggested we could plant a small herb garden and supply the General Store and the local restaurants, Dad patted me on the head and told me it was a nice idea for when I was older. And when I mentioned that the irrigation system in the eastern paddock has been making weird noises for the past month, Oliver told me I was probably hearing things.'

Oliver shifted uncomfortably. 'It hasn't been making weird noises.'

'It has, actually,' Guy said, still focused on his laptop screen. 'Elena noticed it yesterday. Sounds like the pump might need replacing.'

'See? I've been saying that for weeks, but apparently, I don't know enough about the farm to recognise a failing irrigation pump, but Elena does.' Her jaw tightened. 'And not only that. Every day, it's something else I've done wrong, or not done well enough, or should have anticipated before it became a problem. I can't breathe in this house without someone having an opinion about whether I'm doing anything good enough.'

'Mum's just stressed about Dad,' Oliver said, though his voice lacked conviction. 'She doesn't mean—'

'She absolutely means it,' Amelia interrupted. 'And it's not just Mum. I'm tired of making excuses for everyone. I'm tired of being the family scapegoat when things go wrong and the family pet when you need someone to run errands or wash your dishes.'

'If you're so unhappy, what's happened with you moving out?'

'I'm still looking, but trust me, I'm going.' Amelia was horrified that she sounded teary, especially when she saw the look her brothers exchanged.

The sound of the screen door slamming announced Charlotte's arrival, who hurried in, oblivious to the tense atmosphere.

'Great, you're still home, Melie. I want you to—'

'Good morning to you too, *Char*,' Amelia interrupted.

'Oh, sorry. Good morning. I thought I'd call in to see you on the way to school. And please don't call me Char.' Charlotte's words ran together as she walked across and switched the kettle on. 'I'm trying out a new recipe for our dinner party at *Grandmère*'s on Friday night, and I need someone to taste it for me. Can you come over for dinner tonight, Melie?'

'*Amelia*, not Melie. I'm grown up now too, *Charlotte*.'

'I have excellent taste. I'll volunteer,' Oli said.

'I want someone who appreciates good food. You eat peanut butter and banana sandwiches for breakfast,' Charlotte replied with a grin as she reached for the jar of instant coffee. 'Your opinion on Beef Bourguignon is invalid.'

'What about Guy?' Amelia asked, gesturing towards their brother, who was looking hopeful.

'Guy would agree that cardboard was delicious if it meant the conversation ended faster,' Charlotte said matter-of-factly. 'Please, Melie? I really need your help with this. Can you come over?'

Amelia felt the familiar tug of conflicting emotions. On one hand, she was pleased that Charlotte valued her opinion. On the other hand, her assistance was only requested for things like recipes and dresses—never for anything that mattered.

'Tonight?'

Charlotte nodded absently, already assuming that Amelia would do it.

'I can't,' Amelia said, surprising herself with the words. 'I have other plans.'

'What other plans?' Her sister frowned.

'Personal plans,' Amelia replied, lifting her chin slightly.

'What personal plans could you possibly have on a Tuesday night in Duckinwilla Creek?' her sister asked, raising her eyebrows.

'Maybe she has a date,' Guy suggested helpfully, earning himself a glare from Amelia.

'Do you?' Charlotte's expression shifted from irritated to intrigued. 'Wow, who with? Is it someone from Duckinwilla Creek? Do I know him?'

'It's not a date,' Amelia said firmly. 'And even if it was, I don't need to report my social life to the family committee.'

Oliver raised an eyebrow. 'Family committee?'

'You know what I mean,' Amelia said, her earlier frustration returning in full force. 'The way everyone around here thinks they have a right to know every detail of what I'm doing and when I'm doing it, while at the same time treating me like I'm too young to have opinions about anything that matters.'

The words were tumbling out now, fuelled

by months of suppressed resentment and the fresh sting of watching her concerns about Dad being ignored.

'That's not true,' Charlotte protested. 'We just worry about you. You're the baby of the family.'

'No, you all assume things about me,' Amelia corrected. 'There's a difference. You manage me, and you dismiss me, and you assume I'll always be here to pick up the pieces of whatever crisis needs handling while never actually including me in the decisions that affect all of us.'

She flung the tea towel onto the sink and turned to face her siblings. 'You want to know what my plans are? I'm going to look at another rental property in town today. I'm sick of waiting for Mrs Davis to call. She can go whistle! I'll go to the opposition. And I'm sick of living here!'

The stunned silence that followed was so complete that the only sound was the clock ticking in the hallway and the distant sound of Dad's tractor moving between paddocks.

'That's a bit harsh.' Charlotte's voice rose. 'Mum told me she thought you didn't want to move yet. And *Grandmère* agreed with her.'

'So, I've been the subject of discussion, have I? Well, I am moving. And I've applied for the traineeship at the preschool in town, and I'm going to get my own place and start living my own life instead of being the baby sister who gets patted on the head and told to leave the important stuff to the grown-ups.'

Guy's laptop made a small chirping sound that seemed unnaturally loud in the tense kitchen.

'But you can't move out,' Oliver said finally. 'This is home.'

'It will be home when I visit. Like you all do,' Amelia corrected. 'I'm the only one who still lives here, and I'm tired of feeling like this.'

'You're being overdramatic, Melie,' Charlotte said, though her voice lacked its usual certainty.

'Amelia. And am I?' she challenged. 'Tell me the last time anyone treated me like an adult and not Cinderella.'

'You know,' Guy cleared his throat. 'The herb garden idea was pretty good—'

'Too late,' Amelia interrupted. 'Don't try to

make me feel better now by pretending you've suddenly recognised my brilliant contributions. I've made my decision. I'm going.' She headed towards the back door, pausing only to grab her keys from the hook by the window.

'Where are you going now?' Charlotte called after her. 'You need to get changed if you're going to town.'

'Out,' Amelia replied, not turning around. 'I might be back for lunch—Mum's already put your smoko and sandwiches in the fridge—and you boys make sure you clean up after yourselves. And give some thought to Dad. Keep an eye on him while Mum and I are out.'

'Amelia, wait—' Oliver started, but she was already running up the stairs to her room to get changed.

As she climbed into her battered little hatchback a while later—a hand-me-down from Julien that she'd painted bright yellow with purple polka dots, much to the family's horror—Amelia caught sight of her reflection in the rearview mirror. Her hair escaped from its bun in rebellious wisps, her cheeks were flushed with emotion, and her eyes were bright with determination.

For the first time in months, she looked like herself instead of some watered-down version designed to fit her family's expectations.

The drive to town took fifteen minutes along winding roads bordered by sugar cane fields and grazing paddocks. Amelia had made this journey many times, but today it was different—she was driving towards her future instead of just away from her frustrations.

Her first call was to Mrs Henderson, a former resident who had moved to an apartment at the coast when her husband passed away. Even doing that made Amelia feel rebellious.

'Yes, my father's cottage is still available,' the woman responded to Amelia's inquiry. 'It's not a new house. It's quite old, and it needs a tiny bit of work, but it's cute and very comfortable. Would you like to look at it? I'm on my way to Duckinwilla Creek now. I can meet you there if you're interested.'

'Oh, yes, please!'

The old cottage on Maple Street was everything Amelia dreamed of: small but charming, with an overgrown front garden that had potential, and a little back patio that caught the morning sun. The wraparound latticed porch added to the quaint look, and the mature jacaranda tree in the front yard was in full leaf.

Mrs Henderson beamed when Amelia indicated she was happy to move in immediately *if* she was the successful applicant.

'I had another tenant due to move in last weekend, but he didn't arrive, so I'm happy for you to take it.'

'Oh, thank you.' Amelia clasped her hands with happiness.

'You're the youngest Johnson, aren't you?' the older woman asked as they walked through the tiny kitchen with its vintage stone sink and cheerful—albeit stained—yellow walls. 'I met your mother at the CWA meeting a few weeks ago. Even though I've moved, I like to keep up with what's happening in Duckinwilla Creek.'

'Yes, I am.'

'Your brother has done a wonderful job with the General Store. People are talking about it in Bundaberg and Bargara.'

'Yes, we've been getting more tourists in town lately.'

'Your whole family is very community-minded. I heard Julien is going to head the Chamber of Commerce.' That was a surprise to Amelia. 'So, you're looking for a bit of independence? Being a local Johnson is a good enough reference for me.'

'Yes, I am looking forward to having my own space,' Amelia said, surprised at Mrs Henderson's knowledge of her family. Then again, it was Duckinwilla Creek; she should be used to it. 'I'm hoping to start a full-time traineeship at the preschool next month. I have an interview later today.'

Mrs Henderson's face lit up. 'Oh, how wonderful! A community needs local teachers. I do love this valley, but I've found it too hard to be here without my husband. A new start is what I needed, but I can't bring myself to sell the cottage where I grew up.'

'A new start. That's what I'm doing too.'

'And I'm sure you'll be a wonderful tenant. So, Amelia, it's all yours!'

Amelia's head was almost spinning with excitement as ideas for paint colours and furniture arrangements filled her thoughts.

Maybe she could even buy the cottage when she saved enough. 'Are there any conditions? It needs a coat of paint right through. Like, can I paint the walls and choose the colours? Can I add a garden? Maybe put some paintings on the walls?'

'Yes, my only condition is that the house is kept in good condition.'

Amelia's fingers tingled with the itch to get started. The cottage was perfect—small but not cramped, with built-in bookshelves that would hold her large collection of books and high windows that let in the fabulous light. The main bedroom was just big enough for her bed and the vintage dressing table *Grandmère* had given her when they'd left *Maison de Rêve* and moved to their new house a couple of years ago. She sighed with pleasure as she stood at the door to the bathroom; it had one of those clawfoot tubs she'd always dreamed of soaking in with a good book.

Most importantly, it already felt like hers. Not her family home, or someone else's house, and not like a space she was borrowing until she figured out her real life. It felt like home, even with the bland grey walls and bare wooden floors.

By the time Amelia left the cottage an hour later, she had a signed lease agreement in her hand and a move-in date set for the following weekend. Mrs Henderson promised that a handyman and a cleaner would attend to the interior before she moved in.

The afternoon's traineeship interview went equally well, with the director, Mrs Campbell, expressing enthusiasm for Amelia's work ethic, her fresh ideas, and creative approach to early childhood education.

'It's obvious, being a local, that you understand rural needs,' Mrs Campbell had explained. 'Someone who appreciates the children's connection to the land and can incorporate that into their learning experiences. Your family's farming background gives you insights that our city-trained teachers simply don't have.'

Amelia left the preschool having accepted the offer of a three-year fully funded traineeship, a starting date for full-time work that aligned perfectly with her cottage lease, and, for the first time in months, the feeling that someone valued what she had to offer.

It wasn't until she was driving back towards the farm that the enormity of what she'd done began to sink in. In the space of one afternoon, she'd secured her independence and taken the first real steps towards building a new life. Doubt began to settle in her chest, but she forced it down.

The familiar sight of the family farmhouse appearing around the final bend should have felt like coming home, but instead it reassured her; it was a place she was beginning to outgrow.

Her phone buzzed with a text from Charlotte: **Melie, we need to talk. Don't make any hasty decisions. And Greg said he'll taste the beef for me. Love you. Char.**

Amelia smiled as she typed back: **Too late. Already made them.**

Guy and Oliver were sitting on the front porch with a beer, and as she got out of her car, she took a deep breath and prepared to defend the first major decision she'd made entirely on her own.

Everyone had to grow up eventually—even the baby of the Johnson family.

Chapter 2

Four days later, on a crisp autumn morning that made Duckinwilla Valley look like a postcard, Amelia stood on the front porch of 15 Maple Street with her car keys in one hand and a cardboard box balanced on her hip. Several more boxes were on the back seat and in the boot, as well as a suitcase full of clothes, and a huge bag full of her toiletries and hair colours.

The cottage looked as cute as it had during her first visit—but the house and garden certainly needed an enthusiastic tenant with a knack for gardening. She could make it beautiful: she loved gardening and had buckets of enthusiasm.

Most importantly, this was her place now. Her first real home, her entry to independence, and her chance to prove that Amelia Johnson was more than just the baby sister who tasted recipes, swept floors, and washed dishes.

She'd spent the week fielding increasingly creative attempts by her family to change her mind, ranging from Charlotte's guilt trips about abandoning the family during "such a stressful time" to *Grandmère*'s grim predictions about the dangers of young women living alone. Oliver had tried the practical argument about the financial wisdom of staying at home, while Guy had simply shaken his head and muttered something about stubborn Johnson women.

None of them had swayed her determination.

Surprisingly, Mum and Dad had been supportive, and that made leaving a lot easier.

'I do worry about you, Dad,' she said last night as she hugged her father on her last night at home.

'Don't do that, love. I'm just getting older. That heart attack slowed me down.'

'Promise me you'll go for a check-up like Mum wants you to.'

'We'll see.'

Guy had loaded her bed and dressing table onto the farm ute and come to town with her the day before yesterday; he'd carted a sofa and a second-hand table and chairs from St Vinnies, and she'd even got a reluctant smile from him when they'd walked in.

'Not bad at all, Melie, but I think you'll be lonely.'

'Nope. It feels perfect,' she'd said with a smile.

Leaving the farm today had been surprisingly emotional. Amelia had happily packed her belongings—which fitted entirely into her small hatchback with room to spare—but saying goodbye to her childhood bedroom had been harder than expected. Those walls that had witnessed her transformation from the pig-tailed farm kid to a young woman suddenly felt like they were holding all her history.

But as she looked around now, the cottage was even more perfect than she remembered. Sunlight streamed through the large windows, highlighting the built-in bookshelves that would soon hold her collection, and the hardwood floors gleamed with new polish. Her furniture made it look even more homely. The fresh smell of cleaning products met her as she walked from room to room. The compact kitchen had a bunch of fresh herbs in a small jug on the sink, and the living room with the fireplace looked perfect for snuggling with a good book on the second-hand sofa she'd bought.

'Thank you, Mrs Henderson,' she

whispered. Amelia set down the box and took a slow turn around the space, arms outstretched, grinning like an idiot. 'Mine,' she said aloud, just to hear how it sounded. 'All mine. All by myself.'

She spent the morning moving her belongings inside and arranging them, enjoying the freedom of placing her things where she wanted them. As well as sharing the house with five siblings, she and Lisette had shared a bedroom until her sister moved away.

Amelia's books filled the built-in shelves perfectly, Grandmere's emerald and ruby quilt looked beautiful draped over the sofa, and her collection of mismatched dishes from St Vinnie's added cheerful colour to the glass-fronted kitchen cupboards.

By lunchtime, the cottage was beginning to feel like home. Amelia made herself a sandwich using ingredients from her refrigerator, ate at her kitchen table, and grinned the whole time. No one to criticise her, no one to give her chores, no one to dismiss the arrangement of her things.

She was considering where to hang her favourite wall hanging—a vibrant unframed painting of sunflowers that Lisette had created during her brief artistic phase—when the sound of a car pulling into the driveway interrupted her domestic bliss.

Amelia frowned and moved to the front window. She wasn't expecting visitors, and the unfamiliar sedan with New South Wales plates and luggage strapped to the roof didn't belong to anyone she knew.

The car door opened, and a man emerged: a tall, dark-haired stranger. No one she'd ever seen in Duckinwilla Creek before. The designer clothes were obvious as he stood beside the car looking at the cottage.

Amelia watched through the lace curtains as he walked through the unkempt garden towards the front porch, checking a piece of paper in his hand and frowning as he stopped to look at her car. When he started up the front path towards her door, a flutter of unease ran down her back.

The loud knock, when it came, sent another frisson of worry through her.

Amelia opened the door cautiously, keeping the chain latch engaged. 'Can I help you?'

'Bonjour,' the stranger said, offering a smile

that was both charming and slightly uncertain. 'Are you Mrs Henderson? I am supposed to collect the keys for this cottage today.'

Amelia's stomach dropped. 'No, I'm not.'

'The keys for 15 Maple Street,' he clarified, his English accented with the French cadence that she knew very well. 'Which this house is.'

'I think you have the wrong address,' she stuttered, her dreams starting to disintegrate.

'*Non*. I have the lease agreement here.' He pulled a folded paper from his pocket and held it out to her. 'I am Daniel Dupont.'

'There must be some mistake,' Amelia said slowly, a horrible suspicion forming in her mind. 'I'm renting this cottage. I moved in this morning.'

His eyebrows rose in surprise. 'I am sorry, but that is not possible. I have been corresponding with Mrs Henderson about this rental.'

Amelia unlatched the chain and opened the door fully, her mind racing. 'Show me that lease agreement.'

He handed her the paper, and Amelia's heart sank as she recognised Mrs Henderson's writing and what was unmistakably an agreement for 15 Maple Street, with a move-in date of today.

'This can't be right,' she muttered, scanning the document. 'I signed my lease a week ago. She must have been mistaken about your date.'

'May I see your agreement?' he asked politely.

Amelia retrieved her paperwork from the kitchen counter where she'd left it that morning, still glowing with pride at having her own official rental documents. They compared the two leases side by side on her kitchen table, and the reality of the situation became undeniably clear.

Both documents were legitimate. Both bore Mrs Henderson's signature. Both were for the same cottage. And both had move-in dates printed as today.

'Well,' Amelia said faintly, sinking into one of her kitchen chairs. 'This is a stuff-up.'

He took the chair across from her, studying both lease agreements with close attention. 'There must be an error. My agreement was made a week before yours.'

'No, she said you were due here two weeks

ago and didn't arrive.'

'I have been travelling from France.'

Amelia watched him as he spoke. A faint trace of cologne hung in the air between them— it was one of the expensive colognes that Emily stocked in the General Store. His hands moved gracefully as he turned the pages, long fingers with clean, well-kept nails. He was a very good-looking man.

But his voice affected her the most. The French accent should have been familiar by now—with a grandmother who'd insisted that each of her six grandchildren be able to converse in the language—yet something about the way Daniel Dupont shaped his words sent a strange warmth coursing through her. The slight roll of his Rs, the way he pronounced each syllable; it was like listening to music. Even with her worry about the lease, a reluctant flutter of attraction rose.

'Oh, dear,' Amelia said, pushing the paperwork away. She fought the urge to put her head down on the table and cry. After a week of defending her decision to move out, of enduring family doom and gloom about her move, she was now faced with the prospect of having to return to the farm with her tail between her legs on the very first day away. His lease was dated before hers and would probably be the legal one.

'Shit,' she said, and then looked at him apologetically. 'Sorry, it's not your fault.'

His sympathetic smile sent a shiver down to her fingertips.

'Perhaps we should speak to Mrs Henderson?' Daniel suggested. 'I am sure she can resolve this confusion.'

Amelia looked at him again, frustrated that he was handling this bizarre situation with considerably more maturity than she could dig up.

'You're French,' she said, as if that explained something.

'*Oui*—yes,' he confirmed, looking slightly puzzled by her observation.

'And you're here because...?'

He hesitated. 'I am researching. I am hoping to learn about sustainable farming techniques that might apply to our vineyard.'

Well, he's in the right place, Amelia thought. How many times had she heard those words around the kitchen table from Guy and Elana?

She nodded. 'How long were you planning to stay locally?'

'Perhaps a month, perhaps three, depending on my research findings.'

Amelia stared at him, her mind working through the implications. A French wine expert who needed temporary accommodation. A cottage with two bedrooms. And the possibility that there might be an easy solution to Mrs Henderson's stuff-up.

'No, that's insane,' she muttered as she thought it through.

'I beg your pardon?'

'Nothing. I'm just... processing.' She stood up abruptly, pacing to the window and back. 'Where have you been staying until now?'

Daniel looked slightly embarrassed. 'I slept in my rental car at a camping spot north of Brisbane. I arrived here yesterday, and my lease didn't start until today. Mrs Henderson was to meet me here this morning.'

'You've been sleeping in your car?' Amelia turned to stare at him.

'Only one night,' he assured her quickly. 'It

was not ideal, but it was only for a short time. I didn't want to impose on Mrs Henderson. Perhaps I should have called her.'

'She was expecting you two weeks ago.' Amelia frowned. 'Look,' she said suddenly, the words coming out before she could stop them, 'this cottage has two bedrooms.'

Daniel's expression was carefully neutral. 'Yes, I noticed that in the listing.'

'And we both need somewhere to live.'

'We do.'

'Do you have furniture?'

He chuckled. '*Non, je n'ai rien de tel.*'

'I do. So maybe...' Amelia took a deep breath, hardly believing she was about to suggest what she was about to suggest. 'Listen, maybe we could share it. Temporarily. Especially as you only want to be here for a short time.'

Grandmere's clock on the mantle ticked loudly.

Daniel shook his head. 'You would be willing to share accommodation with a stranger?'

'A stranger who makes wine and sleeps in cars rather than imposing on people,' Amelia said. 'That suggests a certain level of character to me.'

'*Ou désespoir*,' he pointed out with what might have been amusement. His lips lifted in a wide smile.

'Well, I'm pretty desperate myself right now,' Amelia admitted. 'I don't want to leave this cottage.'

'Sorry, I must learn more English,' he said. 'But you understood me?'

'I am not unfamiliar with the language.'

'You have travelled to my country?'

'No. I live here. I've moved out of my family's farm for the first time in my life, and leaving here means going home and admitting defeat on day one of my independence experiment.'

'Independence experiment?'

'Long story.' Amelia waved her hand dismissively. 'The point is, we could split the rent, the electricity bill, the household expenses. You'd have accommodation that doesn't involve sleeping in your car, and I get to keep my dignity intact.'

Daniel was quiet for another moment,

considering. 'There would need to be rules,' he said finally. 'I do not have a bed.'

'Well, you can sleep on the floor.' She lifted her chin. 'That's one thing we won't be sharing!'

'Oh, *non*, I did not mean that!'

'I saw one for sale at the op shop in town a couple of days ago.'

'I will go to this op shop and look. But I did mean we need rules. We will be sharing one bathroom and the kitchen.'

'Absolutely,' Amelia agreed quickly. 'We need very clear ground rules about personal space, as well as household responsibilities. And it's completely temporary—for you.' She loved this little cottage, and she was going to stay. After all, she'd been here first and was being kind enough to let him share despite Mrs Henderson's mistake.

'Understood.' Daniel extended his hand across the kitchen table. 'It is a pleasure to meet you. I believe we may have just solved a problem.'

Amelia shook his hand; his grip was firm and warm.

'Amelia Johnson,' she replied. 'Now I need

to call Mrs Henderson and tell her that she made a mistake, but we've come to an agreement.'

He shook his head, and his mouth was set. '*Non*, please let me call her.'

As he pulled out his phone, Amelia stole a glance at her new housemate. Nothing in her life seemed to go to plan.

His dark eyes held hers.

Maybe that wasn't entirely a bad thing.

Wait until she told Lisette she was sharing her house with a handsome Frenchman.

Chapter 3

Daniel came back inside and nodded. 'Mrs Henderson agrees.' That was all he said before he went out to unload his car.

He claimed the smaller bedroom at the back of the cottage, insisting that since Amelia had been there first, she should have the larger room with the better view. He'd put his belongings away quickly, while Amelia spent the same time rearranging her already arranged books for the third time, trying to appear as though the situation was quite normal, before she headed to her room to look at the outline of her TAFE course.

When he'd finished, she heard his car back out of the driveway. When she came out to make a cup of tea and a toasted sandwich, it was dark and there was no sign of Daniel; his door was closed and all was quiet. She looked out through the front door she'd left open for him. His car was back in the driveway.

She took the tea back to her bedroom and closed the door. Was she being too trusting? Should she lock the door? She thought for a moment and then shrugged and went back to her desk.

##

The first twenty-four hours in the same house as Daniel Dupont passed quickly. Their polite interactions in the kitchen and outside the bathroom the next morning would have passed even *Grandmère*'s standards of etiquette. Each of them was very much aware of the other's presence.

The morning routine of the kitchen and shared bathroom was agreed upon amicably. Daniel rose early and made coffee—for both of them—while she showered. They shared breakfast in companionable silence, reading their respective newspapers.

Daniel had somehow procured a French financial paper, while Amelia stuck to the local Bundaberg edition.

'Did you manage to buy that at the local newsagency?' she asked.

'No, it is an old edition. I bought it at the airport.'

'Ah, I see.' She felt very country

bumpkinish reading the local rag, but the conversation remained very civilised.

Very mature.

Very careful.

And the dancing around each other was unsettling Amelia. This was not how she'd imagined being independent would be, but she wouldn't bring her temper and smart mouth from home to this arrangement.

By the third day, they had perfected avoidance. Daniel left each morning with his laptop bag slung over his shoulder. Amelia assumed he was going out to Paterson's; that was the only local vineyard she knew of. The Hendesons' Vineyard had closed when Mr Henderson passed away She wondered why he was here in Duckinwilla Valley. Surely the Barossa or Hunter Valley vineyards would be more suitable for a French visitor?

She shrugged as she turned back to her workbook; it was none of her business. Once his car had backed out of the driveway, she buried herself in her TAFE coursework at the kitchen table, spreading textbooks and notes across the surface. When evening approached, she listened for the sound of his car in the driveway, trying to time her movements to avoid him.

They nearly collided in the hallway that night—Daniel walking quietly down the hall, Amelia emerging from the bathroom with her hair wrapped in a towel. Both froze, then executed an awkward sideways shuffle, each trying to give the other maximum space in the narrow corridor.

'Sorry,' they said simultaneously, then stopped, looking anywhere but at each other.

'I was just—' Amelia began.

'Of course, I'll just—' Daniel gestured vaguely towards his room.

The polite one step left, one step right continued into the kitchen, where they moved around each other awkwardly, each aware of where the other was stepping.

'You don't have to ask permission to use the kitchen,' she finally snapped a while later as Daniel hovered uncertainly in the doorway for the third time since he'd arrived home.

He paused in the act of checking his watch—again—and gave her a quizzical look. 'I was simply ensuring I wasn't interrupting your dinner preparations.'

'It's a *shared* kitchen,' Amelia pointed out, perhaps more sharply than necessary. 'That means we both get to use it without conducting a formal negotiation every time we want to open the fridge.'

'Of course,' Daniel agreed, though he still didn't move from the doorway. 'I was merely wishing to be considerate.'

'You're being too considerate,' Amelia said, abandoning her attempt to cook pasta. 'While I appreciate your consideration, it's not natural. I can't live like this, watching my every move. This isn't working.'

Daniel's eyebrows rose. 'The living arrangement isn't working? It's only been—'

'The politeness isn't working,' Amelia clarified, gesturing with her wooden spoon and sending droplets of pasta sauce across the counter. 'All this tiptoeing around each other and pretending we're invisible. It's exhausting me.'

'I see.' Daniel finally entered the kitchen, moving to the sink to wash his hands. 'What do you suggest we do instead?'

Amelia considered this as she stirred her

sauce. 'How about we try acting like normal people who share a living space, instead of trying to stay out of each other's way? It's too small a space to do that. And at this rate, you won't eat until midnight.'

'Normal people,' Daniel repeated thoughtfully. 'How do normal people behave in shared houses?'

'They argue about whose turn it is to do the dishes,' Amelia replied promptly. 'They steal each other's leftovers and complain about whose turn it is to clean, and then they hog the bathroom during peak hours.'

Daniel tilted his head, but a smile played around his lips. Amelia forced herself to look away as that attraction hit her again. Maybe that's why she was doing her best to avoid him?

'Hog... like the pig?' he said. 'Are you telling me that Australian housemates bring farm animals into the bathroom? Perhaps I should have been warned about this.'

'No, I'm talking about household chores.'

'You wish to argue about household chores?'

'I wish to stop walking on eggshells.'

Amelia lifted her eyes to his face again. 'Look, this arrangement is weird enough without us both pretending it's completely normal. Can we at least acknowledge that it's strange and figure out how to make it work without all the yes, sir, no, sir, three bags full, sir?'

Daniel's expression shifted from confusion to something approaching amusement. 'I don't understand what you just said, but from your tone, I believe you think we're being ridiculous.' He gestured between them. 'And perhaps you're right.'

'It's called "*Baa Baa Black Sheep*",' Amelia explained, feeling slightly foolish. 'It's a nursery rhyme. The sheep just keeps agreeing to everything—"yes, sir, yes, sir, three bags full". That's what we're doing. Being overly polite and accommodating instead of just... living normally.'

Daniel's mouth quirked upward at one corner. 'Ah. So, I am the sheep in this scenario?'

'We both are,' Amelia said. 'Dancing around each other like we're afraid the other might bite.'

'Well,' Daniel said, stepping fully into the

kitchen and opening the refrigerator. 'I can assure you I don't bite. Though I cannot speak for you.'

Amelia burst out giggling as a memory of biting Oli when she was a toddler surfaced—still legendary in the annals of Johnson family history. 'Perhaps,' she said, still laughing, 'I did once, so I can't promise anything.'

Daniel's eyebrows rose, and something decidedly wicked flickered in his dark eyes. 'Well then,' he said, his voice dropping to a lower register, 'I suppose I'll have to be very careful about which parts of myself I put within reach.'

The air in the kitchen suddenly crackled with tension, and heat crept up Amelia's neck as she realised the direction his mind had wandered. She opened her mouth to say something—anything—but found herself just staring at him instead.

Daniel seemed to realise what he'd implied at the same moment, and he cleared his throat, a faint flush appearing on his cheekbones. 'I meant... fingers. For cooking. Obviously.'

'Of course,' Amelia echoed weakly, though

neither of them looked at the other.

'In that case,' Daniel said, moving to the refrigerator, 'I am now going to prepare my dinner without requesting your approval. And I might even use more than one burner on the stove.'

'Scandalous,' Amelia declared, but she was smiling too.

The difference was immediate. Within minutes, they'd fallen into a kind of easy kitchen routine. Daniel proved to be an excellent cook—the way he handled a knife suggested he knew his way around a kitchen—while Amelia contributed *Grandmère*'s secret to perfect pasta water and her talent for finding exactly the right herbs in the overgrown garden.

'Where did you learn to cook like that?' Amelia asked, watching Daniel prepare what appeared to be a professional-quality sauce with ingredients he'd somehow produced from his single bag of groceries.

'*Grandmère*,' Daniel replied, as he quickly diced carrots. 'She insisted that all her grandchildren learn to feed themselves properly. "*Une personne qui ne sait pas faire la cuisine,*" she would say, "*est une personne qui dépendra toujours des autres*".'

'A person who cannot cook will always be dependent on others,' Amelia observed. '*Grandmère* says something similar, except she focuses more on the social aspects. "*La nourriture rassemble les gens*," and all that.'

Daniel's knife paused mid-chop, and he looked up at her with genuine surprise. 'You speak my language very well.'

'A little,' Amelia said, trying to sound casual despite the pleased flush that warmed her cheeks at his expression. 'We grew up surrounded by the language, plus I took it through high school.'

'Your accent is perfect,' he said, and there was something in his voice—approval? interest?—that made her stomach do a small flip. 'I wasn't expecting...'

'What? That a country girl from Duckinwilla Creek might know a second language?' she teased, though not unkindly. 'Among other things.' Amelia relaxed as they talked, the strange tension of the past days finally beginning to dissipate. '*Grandmère* grew up in France. Married an Australian and moved here with nothing but her recipes and her opinions.'

'Ah,' Daniel said with understanding. 'A woman of strong character.'

'That's one way to put it.' Amelia laughed. '*Grandmère*'s been running the Johnson family with an iron fist disguised as French charm for sixty years. Nothing happens on the family farm without her approval.'

'And she approved of your move to independence?'

Amelia's smile faltered slightly. 'She'll adjust. *Grandmère* has very traditional views about young women living alone.'

'But not about young women pursuing their ambitions?'

The perceptiveness of the question caught Amelia off guard. 'How do you know I have ambitions beyond escaping my family's dinner table?'

Daniel shrugged, casually adding wine to the sauce. 'You left the family home to take a risk on the unknown.'

'Maybe I'm just tired of being treated like the family mascot,' Amelia said, though she was surprised by how accurately he'd assessed her motivations.

'Perhaps,' Daniel agreed. 'But mascots rarely sign leases and start new careers. They simply complain about their circumstances without changing them.'

Amelia paused in her pasta stirring to study his profile. 'You seem to know a lot about family dynamics.'

'Large families are the same everywhere,' Daniel said, waving the knife in the air. 'Birth order, expectations, trying to establish your place in the family, always governed by who's the oldest and the youngest.'

'Sounds like you're speaking from experience.'

Daniel's hands stilled for just a moment before resuming the steady chopping. A small bowl was now filled with carrot, onion, and potato. 'Perhaps.'

Amelia almost pushed for him to explain, but something in his hesitation warned her off. Instead, she focused on the change in their sharing of space. Where ten minutes ago they'd been circling each other like wary cats, now they moved together easily—Daniel reaching around her for the pepper mill just as she stepped aside to check her pasta, Amelia handing him a clean spoon when he turned.

'This is better,' she observed, surprised by how natural it felt.

'Much better,' Daniel agreed. 'Though I should warn you, my morning routine includes playing music. Classical, mostly, but sometimes jazz if I'm feeling adventurous.'

'I sing in the shower,' Amelia countered. 'Loudly. And not often in tune if you believe my brothers.'

'I leave coffee cups everywhere,' Daniel admitted.

'I reorganise everything when I'm stressed,' Amelia confessed. 'Books, groceries, spice racks, bathroom supplies—nothing is safe from my anxiety-driven tidying sprees.'

'I talk to myself when I'm working through problems,' Daniel said. 'Usually in French.'

'I paint my nails different colours when I'm bored,' Amelia replied. 'Last week I did rainbow stripes. It was either that or dye my hair purple again.'

Daniel glanced at her current blue and silver

locks. 'You consider purple a significant escalation?'

'Purple would have required more bleaching first,' Amelia explained seriously. 'It's a bigger commitment.'

They both laughed, and Amelia realised that the nervous energy that had been humming through her system since Saturday finally began to settle. This strange arrangement might actually work—not because they were perfectly compatible, but because they were both willing to figure out how to get it to work.

She opened her mouth to say that and then thought twice.

Don't be impulsive.

'So,' she said as they sat down to eat together. 'What exactly are you hoping to learn in Duckinwilla Creek that you can't figure out from French vineyards?'

Daniel waved a casual hand. 'Many things. I believe Australian farmers have developed innovative approaches.'

'Sounds like important work,' Amelia said. 'How did you end up being the one to travel halfway around the world for research?'

Daniel's fork paused halfway to his mouth. 'I had the most flexibility in my schedule.'

It was another deflection, polite but unmistakable. Amelia filed away her growing curiosity about what Daniel Dupont wasn't telling her about his circumstances.

'What about you?' Daniel asked, smoothly redirecting the conversation. 'You mentioned starting a new job. Teaching?'

'Preschool. I've been there part-time. Now I have a traineeship and I'm full-time.' Amelia confirmed, grateful for the safer topic. 'Four-year-olds who think I'm the most interesting person they've ever met because I have blue hair and know all the words to "*The Wheels on the Bus*".'

'You enjoy working with children?'

'I love it,' Amelia said, surprised by the fervour in her voice. 'They're honest and curious and haven't learned yet that some questions aren't supposed to be asked. Plus, they don't care that I'm the youngest in my family or that maybe I don't know as much as they think I do. To them, I'm just Miss Amelia who knows interesting facts about butterflies and makes excellent playdough from scratch.'

'Miss Amelia,' Daniel repeated with a small smile. 'It suits you.'

'Better than "Melie" or "the baby" or "Hugo's youngest",' Amelia agreed. 'I'm looking forward to being known for what I do rather than whose sister or daughter I am.'

'A noble goal,' Daniel said seriously.

'Is that what you're doing?' Amelia asked. 'Trying to be known for yourself?'

Daniel's face closed, and he looked away.

Whoops, overstepped the mark again.

'No, I'm simply doing my job,' he said.

'Right,' Amelia agreed, though she'd definitely hit something sensitive. 'Sorry. I didn't mean to assume. My family's always telling me I often start on the wrong foot.'

'No need to apologise,' Daniel assured her with a chuckle. 'And that is an interesting expression.'

By the time they'd cleaned up the kitchen together, the awkwardness had passed, and Amelia vowed to herself not to pry again.

'Thank you for dinner,' Daniel said as they finished drying the last of the dishes. Your sauce was excellent.'

'Thank you for not letting me burn the pasta,' Amelia replied.

They stood in the kitchen for a moment, and the silence stretched just long enough to become awkward again before Daniel cleared his throat.

'I have some work to do before bed,' he said. 'If you'll excuse me.'

'Of course,' Amelia agreed quickly. 'I've got lesson plans to work on too.'

Daniel headed towards his room, pausing at the doorway to look back. 'Amelia? Thank you. For suggesting we try to be normal people instead of diplomats. It was... good advice.'

'You're welcome,' she said. 'Same time tomorrow? For the whole coexisting thing?'

'Same time tomorrow,' Daniel confirmed with a wide grin.

After he'd disappeared into his room, Amelia cleaned the kitchen one more time— not because it needed it, but because cleaning helped her think. The evening had been a success— mostly. They'd shared space without getting in each other's way, discovered that they both could cook, and that conversation between them didn't have to be awkward.

While ever I don't overstep the mark.

Daniel Dupont had made it clear that his personal life was off-limits. Which was fine, she told herself firmly. They were temporary housemates, not confidants. Everyone was entitled to their privacy.

Still, as she went back to her room, she couldn't shake her curiosity about what Daniel wouldn't share. She pulled out her phone and opened FaceTime, scrolling to Lisette's contact. Her sister's face appeared on screen moments later.

'Well, well,' Lisette said immediately. 'What have you done to your hair? Those colours are very subdued… for you.'

'Thanks for noticing the important things first,' Amelia said dryly. 'And before you ask, yes, I got the traineeship. And yes, I've moved out.'

'I know.' Lisette's expression softened. '*Grandmère* rang in a complete state. Then Charlotte called me. They're both worried sick.'

Amelia spent the next five minutes explaining why she'd moved out. Lisette listened with her usual mixture of scepticism and understanding.

'I think you'll be fine,' she said. 'As long as you visit home and *Grandmère*, and you don't get too lonely by yourself.'

Amelia hesitated. 'Okay, I have a secret, but you're not to tell anyone.'

Lisette's eyes lit up. 'Ooooh, what?'

'Promise me.'

'I promise, now spill.'

Amelia told her about Daniel, about the arrangement, about how it had all come about. Lisette's eyebrows climbed higher as Amelia described what a good-looking guy he was.

'You know Mrs. Henderson knows,' Lisette said when Amelia finished. 'And you know she'll tell someone when she's back in town.'

'I know.'

'I bet *Grandmère* taps at your front door tomorrow.'

After they hung up, Amelia stared at the ceiling, wondering what on earth she'd say if *Grandmère* did turn up.

Chapter 4

The doorbell rang at precisely seven-thirty the next morning, which should have been Amelia's first warning that her new life was about to implode.

She padded to the front door in her favourite pyjamas—the ones with tiny koalas printed on pale blue cotton that Lisette had given her last Christmas, with the comment that they were "adorably daggy" and would suit her. Her heart sank when she peered through the peephole.

Grandmère stood on the front step, handbag clutched in one hand and a covered casserole dish balanced in the other, looking like a woman on a mission. She was dressed in her "visiting" outfit: navy slacks, cream blouse, and the pearls that had belonged to her mother. Her silver hair was perfectly styled despite the early hour, and her posture suggested she'd been awake and battle-ready since dawn.

'*Merde*,' Amelia whispered, then immediately felt guilty for swearing in French as though *Grandmère* might somehow psychically detect it.

The doorbell rang again, followed by a sharp rap that brooked no argument.

'Amélie, *ma chérie*, I know you are home. Open this door immediately.'

Amelia glanced desperately towards the hallway, hoping against hope that Daniel was still asleep and might remain so until this visit concluded. No such luck. She could hear the shower running in the bathroom, and worse, the rich scent of freshly brewed coffee wafting from the kitchen suggested he'd already begun their morning routine.

'Coming, *Grandmère*,' she called, plastering on what she hoped was a convincing smile before opening the door. 'What a lovely surprise! You're up early this morning.'

'As are you, apparently.' *Grandmère*'s narrowed blue eyes took in Amelia's pyjamas, her sleep-mussed hair, and the general air of domestic morning chaos. 'May I come in? This dish is quite heavy.'

'Of course, of course.' Amelia stepped aside, her mind racing through damage control strategies. 'I was just about to make breakfast. Would you like some coffee?'

'That would be lovely.' *Grandmère* stepped into the hallway and immediately began her inspection, taking in the two sets of keys hanging by the door, the jacket draped over the hall chair, and the distinctly masculine cologne that lingered in the air. 'I see you have settled in well.'

'Very well, thank you. The cottage is perfect for my needs.'

'And apparently for other needs as well,' *Grandmère* observed mildly, setting her casserole dish on the hall table and fixing Amelia with a look that had brought Johnson family members to confession for sixty years.

The shower stopped running.

Amelia's smile became increasingly strained. 'What's in the dish? It smells wonderful.'

'*Coq au vin*. I thought you might appreciate a proper meal, given your... circumstances.' *Grandmère*'s pause before "circumstances" could have sunk a battleship. 'Shall we go to the kitchen? I should very much like to meet your housemate.'

'Oh, he's probably still asleep,' Amelia said

desperately, leading the way towards the kitchen while frantically trying to think of an escape plan. 'You know how men can be in the morning. Very slow to wake up. Could be hours before he emerges.'

The kitchen looked cosy and domesticated. Two coffee cups sat on the counter, steam still rising from both. The morning paper lay folded beside Daniel's place at the table, while Amelia's TAFE textbooks were stacked neatly at her regular place at the table. A half-eaten piece of toast on a plate suggested someone had been interrupted mid-breakfast.

Grandmère took it in with a single sweep of her gaze.

'How... cosy,' she murmured, settling herself at the table with the air of someone prepared to stay until all secrets were revealed. 'And how long have you been sharing this domestic bliss?'

'It's not domestic bliss, it's just practical— and platonic, *Grandmère*,' Amelia said quickly, pouring coffee into a third cup and adding the precise amount of milk *Grandmère* preferred. 'We barely see each other, really. Ships passing in the night and all that.'

'Ships that share breakfast and morning papers, I see.'

Footsteps sounded in the hallway, accompanied by what was unmistakably masculine humming—a cheerful tune that suggested Daniel was having a perfectly pleasant morning until he walked into the kitchen.

He appeared in the doorway, hair still damp from his shower, wearing dark jeans and a pale blue shirt that brought out his eyes. He stopped short when he saw *Grandmère*, but recovered a reaction that spoke of considerable practice dealing with unexpected situations.

'*Bonjour, madame,*' he said, offering a slight bow. 'You must be Amelia's *Grandmère*. I am Daniel Dupont. *Enchanté de faire votre connaissance.*'

Grandmère tilted her head to the side and her eyebrows rose a fraction—whether it was his perfect pronunciation or simply his good looks, Amelia couldn't tell.

'Monsieur Dupont,' *Grandmère* replied in flawless French. '*Quel plaisir inattendu. Votre français est excellent.*'

'*Merci, madame. Ma famille est de Lyon, mais j'ai grandi à Paris.*'

'Ah, Paris. *Une belle ville. Et que faites-vous en Australie, si ce n'est pas indiscret*?'

Grandmère's polite conversation was her way of conducting a full interrogation. Daniel was holding his own admirably, but she could see the slight tension around his eyes that suggested he was choosing his words carefully.

Amelia straightened and took a deep breath. This was not going to happen. How dare her family do this? Sending *Grandmère* at some ungodly hour of the morning in an attempt to catch her out. Well, there was nothing to be gained by allowing this to continue. Her temper began to build; she was just getting to know Daniel, and she liked him. Now her family was going to make her look like a little girl who needed supervision.

She swallowed and opened her mouth to speak; no one challenged *Grandmère*, but she was about to.

'I work in agricultural research.' Daniel switched to English with a glance towards Amelia before she could get the words out. 'I am here studying innovative farming techniques. Your granddaughter has been most helpful in assisting me to find a home.'

'I'm sure she has,' *Grandmère* said dryly, also switching to English. 'Amelia has always been... generous with her hospitality. Are you still seeing your young man?'

'*Grandmère*!' Amelia said. 'You know very well that I am not.'

'Would you care for coffee, Monsieur Dupont?' *Grandmère* continued as if Amelia hadn't spoken. 'We are so pleased to see Amelia settling into her new independent life so... thoroughly.'

Grandmère watched Daniel move to the coffee pot and reach for his mug.

'You seem very much at home here,' she observed.

'Amelia has made me feel most welcome,' Daniel replied carefully. 'It is not easy, finding oneself in a new country with unfamiliar customs. She has been... how do you say... a good mate?'

The slight questioning inflection as he used the Australian term was perfectly pitched to suggest someone still learning the language, but Amelia caught the glint of humour in his eyes. He was enjoying this. Her irritation grew.

'A good mate,' *Grandmère* repeated thoughtfully. 'How fortunate for you both.' She then settled back in her chair. 'And your family, Monsieur Dupont? Are they also in agriculture?'

'In a manner of speaking. My father works in agricultural technology, developing new systems for crop management. My mother is a food scientist. They met at university.'

'How romantic. And they approve of your... research journey to Australia?'

Daniel's pause was barely perceptible, but Amelia caught it. 'They understand my desire to improve my knowledge.'

'Naturally. And how long do you anticipate this research will take?'

Another pause, even briefer. 'These things are difficult to predict. One must be thorough.'

'Well,' *Grandmère* said brightly, 'I do hope you'll have time to experience some Australian culture while you're here. Amelia, you must take Monsieur Dupont to the Bundaberg Distillery. And perhaps a Sunday lunch at the farm? I'm sure your parents would be delighted to meet him.'

'Oh, that's not necessary—' Amelia began.

'I would be honoured.' Amelia stared when Daniel interrupted. 'I have heard about your family's farm. I would be interested to see traditional Australian agricultural methods firsthand.'

Grandmère's smile was triumphant. 'Excellent. Shall we say this Sunday? Nothing formal, just family.'

Amelia shook her head. 'I have plans for Sunday.' She wasn't going to tell them that her plans involved a new hair colour and ironing her clothes for the week at work.

'Nonsense. Change them, Amelia. I insist. It's been far too long since we've had an interesting dinner guest.' *Grandmère* rose from her chair. 'And now I must be going. I have a Garden Club meeting at nine.'

Daniel stood and accompanied her to the door.

'Monsieur Dupont, it has been a pleasure,' she said, offering her hand with regal grace. 'I look forward to continuing our conversation on

Sunday.'

'As do I, madame,' Daniel replied, taking her hand and executing another perfect bow. 'Until Sunday.'

Grandmère turned to Amelia, and her expression softened slightly. '*Ma chérie*, take care of yourself. Your family misses you.'

She kissed Amelia's cheek, leaving behind the familiar scent of Chanel No. 5, and then sailed out the front door.

Amelia closed the door and leaned against it.

'Well,' Daniel said mildly, 'that was interesting.'

'She is a busybody,' Amelia said flatly. 'She knows everything. She probably knew before she walked through that door.'

'Knew what, exactly?' Daniel's wary eyes held hers.

'That we're not just housemates. That we were becoming friends.' She gestured vaguely between them. '*Grandmère* likes to be in control. I apologise. I should have taken a rental hundreds of kilometres away if I really wanted to succeed in being independent. I'm sorry your day started off like that.'

Daniel was quiet for a moment, and then he chuckled. 'Your *Grandmère* seems like a perceptive woman. She is very much like mine.'

'Perceptive? You have no idea. She's going to spend the next week conducting a full background investigation. By Sunday, she'll know your blood type, your credit rating, and probably your mother's maiden name.'

Daniel laughed, and the sound sent a warm flutter through her chest. 'In that case, I shall look forward to Sunday.'

'Daniel,' Amelia said seriously, 'you don't understand. Sunday lunch with my family isn't just a meal. You can't go. I have no intention of kowtowing to them. It will be a trial by fire. They're going to assume we're... that you're...'

'Your boyfriend?'

Amelia's cheeks burned. 'Something like that.'

'And would that be such a terrible thing? For them to think so, I mean.'

She looked at him standing there in her hallway, hair still damp, eyes warm with what might have been an invitation, and that warmth coiled in her stomach. A week ago, her biggest concern had been whether she could find a rental. Now she was fielding questions about fake boyfriends and fighting real attraction; the careful independence she'd worked so hard to achieve was already at risk thanks to her interfering family. She wasn't going to examine this attraction to Daniel. It was different from what she'd felt before—more mature—and it wasn't as though she hadn't had a boyfriend.

His eyes held hers. 'Perhaps we could play them at their own game?'

Amelia frowned. 'What do you mean?'

'Well, I am assuming that the early morning visit was calculated to catch you out, if indeed you did have a secret boyfriend in your house?'

'Exactly!'

'And they will expect you to deny that?'

'Yes.'

'Do you really have other plans for Sunday?'

Amelia pulled a face. 'Not really.'

'Well then, let's go to lunch and give them a shock. My family is exactly like this, and I know how to handle them. Can you act?'

Amelia nodded slowly, and a smile tilted her lips. 'I can.'

She didn't tell Daniel that it wouldn't be hard to act as though she was his girlfriend.

Sunday lunch with her family was going to be interesting; she was already looking forward to it.

Chapter 5

The phone rang early on Sunday morning, just as Amelia and Daniel were discussing an excuse for not going to Grandmere's for lunch.

'Hello, *Grandmère.*'

Amelia caught Daniel's eye, and he shook his head almost imperceptibly. They'd managed to postpone the dreaded Sunday lunch for the past two weekends, but he knew they wouldn't be able to for a third time.

Amelia nodded at Daniel as she listened. 'You must be psychic, *Grandmère.* I just picked up the phone to call you.'

Daniel moved over and stood behind her, his hands settling on her shoulders. The warmth of her skin beneath his fingers sent a pleasant quiver down his spine. 'Daniel's got a bit of a sore throat, and he doesn't want to risk sharing it.'

He grinned, coughing a little in the background.

Amelia listened again and then nodded. 'Next Sunday, for sure. I'll make sure he looks after himself. No, don't worry about dropping your chicken soup in. I'll look after him.'

She listened for a few minutes longer. 'Yes, love you too, *Grandmère*. See you soon.'

Daniel held up her coffee cup as she disconnected. 'More coffee?'

'Yes, please. I need to get the taste of guilt out of my mouth. You know, she didn't believe a word of what I said.'

'So,' Daniel said, topping up her cup. 'What does a miraculously recovered man do with his unexpected Sunday freedom?'

Amelia pressed her back against the kitchen counter, watching him. Three weeks. Had it really only been such a short time since Daniel moved in?

'Beach?' she suggested.

His face lit up, and he nodded.

'I know just the place.'

Their weekend drives had started innocently enough. Amelia had mentioned the beach one morning over coffee, and Daniel said he'd love to explore. She offered to show him her favourite places. His rental car had dodgy air conditioning, so they drove with windows down, her hair whipping everywhere while she pointed out landmarks

'That old house there—see the blue shutters? The woman who lives there keeps peacocks,' she said, gesturing towards a weathered cottage set back from the road. 'I can hear them calling in the mornings when I drive past. Next turn left,' she said.

Daniel pulled into a scrubby car park she'd visited hundreds of times as a teenager. 'Tourists stick to the main beach. This is where the locals come.'

The path down to the water was steep and narrow, winding between tea trees and coastal scrub. Daniel went first, turning back to offer his hand when the track got particularly rocky. His hand was warm, and he didn't let go even when they reached easier ground.

The beach was a small crescent of sand tucked between two rocky headlands, almost empty except for an elderly man walking his dog near the water's edge. The black rocks of the Capricornia coast jutted dramatically from the water, weathered smooth by decades of salt spray. The waves were gentle here, protected by the curve of the bay, and the sand was soft and pale.

'It's a perfect beach,' Amelia said.

'It's more private than the one I discovered last week after I visited—when I came to town. I sat there for two hours,' he said, drawing patterns in the sand with his finger. 'Just thinking.'

'What were you thinking about?'

'Whether I wanted to stay here.'

'And?' she asked quietly.

'Still figuring that out,' he said, but his eyes, when they met hers, suggested he might be closer to an answer than he'd been two weeks ago.

***

Walking back to the car, Amelia pointed to the small store at the top of the hill. 'I could go an ice-cream.'

'Wait here,' Daniel said, and hurried up the hill without giving her a chance to protest.

He came back with two Magnums, handing her the caramel one like he'd been buying her ice cream forever.

'How did you know this was my favourite?' she asked, peeling away the wrapper.

'You had one in your freezer the first week I moved in. Seemed like a safe bet.'

They ate their ice creams leaning against his

car, and Amelia watched as the breeze ruffled his hair. It was hard to believe she was at her favourite beach, eating ice-cream with a drop-dead gorgeous Frenchman.

'What?' he asked, catching her stare.

'Nothing,' she said quickly, focusing intently on her ice cream.

He stepped closer, close enough that she had to tilt her head back to meet his eyes. 'You've got a bit of caramel here,' he said softly, his thumb brushing the corner of her mouth.

The touch was feather-light, over almost before it began, but sent electricity shooting through her entire body.

'There,' Daniel said, his voice rougher than usual. 'All clean.'

Movie nights had crept up on them, too, evolving from a casual suggestion to something Amelia looked forward to all day. It started the week after Daniel moved in, when she'd fallen asleep on the couch during some action movie he was watching. She'd woken up with his jacket draped over her shoulders and the TV volume turned down low, Daniel nowhere to be seen.

The next evening, he'd asked what she wanted to watch.

'Don't care,' she'd said, which was a lie. She cared about sitting next to him on her couch, close enough to smell his soap and feel the warmth coming off his skin. She cared about the way he made little comments during movies, observations that were funnier than the actual comedy they were supposed to be watching.

Tonight felt different, though. The day at the beach had changed something between them.

'Your pick tonight,' Daniel said, settling onto the couch with a bowl of popcorn balanced on his lap.

Amelia curled up beside him, closer than usual, and scrolled through the options on Netflix. His arm stretched along the back of the couch behind her, not quite touching but close enough that she could feel the warmth radiating from his skin. Each rise and fall of his chest seemed loud in the quiet room, a steady rhythm that made her breathing shallow.

'This one,' she said, selecting something at random.

Twenty minutes in, she realised she'd

chosen a romantic comedy from the nineties, all longing glances and sexual tension. On screen, the leads were having their first kiss, and the living room suddenly felt very small.

'We could watch something else,' Daniel offered, but his voice was distracted, and when Amelia looked at him, his attention was on her rather than the television.

'It's fine,' she said, but the words came out breathier than she intended.

They were sitting closer now, though she couldn't remember either of them moving. Daniel's fingers were playing with a strand of her hair, the touch so light she almost wondered if she was imagining it.

'Amelia,' he said quietly.

'Yeah?'

'I'm glad we skipped lunch today. I really enjoyed myself.'

She turned to face him fully, tucking one leg under herself. 'Me too.'

'We can't keep making excuses forever.'

'I know.' She studied his face in the flickering light from the TV. 'Are you worried about being interrogated?'

Daniel was quiet for a long moment. 'I'm worried about what happens after that.'

'What do you mean?'

'It will put pressure on me to make a decision.' The honesty in his voice took her breath away. On screen, the credits were rolling, but neither of them moved to find something else to watch.

'For what it's worth,' Amelia said finally, 'I don't think any decisions need to be made in a hurry.'

Daniel's hand found her face, his thumb tracing the line of her cheekbone. 'No?'

'No,' she whispered.

He leaned forward, and when he kissed her, it was slow, deliberate, and full of intention. When they finally broke apart, both breathing hard, Amelia knew they'd crossed another line— one that led somewhere neither of them had planned to go.

'Don't go back to your room,' she said against his lips.

Daniel pulled back just enough to search her eyes. 'Are you sure?'

Instead of answering with words, Amelia

took his hand and led him down the hallway, the forgotten movie credits playing to an empty room.

Chapter 6

Early the next morning, Daniel stared at his laptop screen, the cursor blinking accusingly in the empty email field. Outside, Amelia's car was backing down the driveway—she was going to her preschool. The house felt strangely quiet after the night they'd spent together, after crossing the line from housemates to something more.

He could still smell her lemon shampoo on his pillow, still feel the weight of her head against his shoulder. They'd talked until nearly dawn, sharing stories and secrets in the darkness, her hand resting on his chest as if she belonged there. When she'd finally fallen asleep, he'd lain awake watching her breathe, marvelling at how right it felt to have her curled against him.

But now, in the harsh light of morning and with the demands of his real life intruding via email, doubt crept in. What was he doing? Three weeks ago, he'd been Daniel Dupont, rising star of international agricultural acquisition, focused solely on closing the Henderson deal. Now he was lying awake thinking about a woman's laugh, about morning coffee conversations, about the possibility of a future he'd never planned.

His phone buzzed with an incoming video call from Marcus Chen, his colleague and the closest thing he had to a best friend. Daniel accepted the call, and Marcus' familiar face appeared on screen, looking harried.

'Finally,' Marcus said without preamble. 'I've been trying to reach you for two days. Please tell me you've made progress with the acquisition.'

Daniel ran a hand through his hair, a gesture that Marcus would recognise as hesitation. 'It's more complex than we anticipated.'

'How complex? Because Jean is breathing down my neck about the timeline, and the board is starting to ask pointed questions about why you're taking so long to close what should have been a straightforward purchase.'

'The technology is exactly what we thought it was,' Daniel said carefully. 'Revolutionary soil analysis capabilities, potential to transform crop yields across our vineyards. But Mrs Henderson is... not sure she wants to sell.'

'Why?'

Daniel thought about his conversations with Eleanor Henderson, the way she'd studied him with shrewd eyes when he'd gone to Bargara yesterday and made the offer on her vineyard.

'I'm not sure it's for sale. She said her husband is still very much a part of that land for her.' Daniel had understood her emotion as they looked out over the vines.

Marcus frowned. 'Can't we just increase the offer? Everyone has a price.'

'This isn't about money,' Daniel said, then immediately regretted the sharp edge in his voice. Marcus was a good friend and an excellent business partner, but he'd never understood that some things couldn't be solved with money.

'Everything is about money eventually,' Marcus replied. 'Look, I know you're enjoying being in Australia, but we have investors to answer to. How much longer do you need?'

Daniel's jaw tightened at the casual dismissal. 'If I rush it, we could lose the deal.'

'We need a definitive timeline. The office can only cover for you for so long, and frankly, the boss is starting to wonder if you're considering this as a holiday.'

'I don't like that assumption, Marcus. It took me weeks of touring around before I stumbled on this place. As you know, it was that lead in the Hunter vineyards that led me here. I just can't walk in and expect the owner to agree to sell. And I'm not one hundred per cent sure it's the technology we've been chasing.'

'Work harder, Daniel.' Marcus ended the call, and Daniel sat staring at the blank screen. He wasn't lying, exactly—the Henderson acquisition was complex, and Mrs Henderson was very particular about her late husband's legacy. The truth was, he'd been finding excuses to extend his stay, telling himself it was about further investigation of Henderson's technology when it was really the woman who made terrible jokes while cooking dinner and sang off-key in the shower who was filling his thoughts day and night. He'd only been here a short time; how could he fall for someone so quickly?

Chapter 7

The sound of a car door slamming interrupted his brooding. Daniel glanced out the window, expecting to see Amelia returning, but the car parked behind his was unfamiliar. A tall woman emerged, her movements purposeful as she strode towards the front door.

The doorbell rang twice in quick succession.

'You must be the mysterious Daniel,' she said when he opened the door. 'I'm Charlotte, Amelia's sister. Is she home?'

'She's at school,' Daniel replied, stepping aside to let her in. 'She's not been gone long.'

He'd been pleased that Marcus had called after Amelia left. They had chatted and laughed over breakfast, and she'd seemed reluctant to leave as they lingered over a second coffee. He had kissed her goodbye and she had lingered as long as she could.

'Perfect. That gives us time to talk.' Charlotte stepped inside. 'Is that coffee I can smell?'

'Of course.' Daniel followed her to the kitchen, amused. These Johnson women were confident. 'I take it this visit is not entirely social?'

'Nothing about this situation is social,' Charlotte settled herself at the kitchen table, and he thought how much she resembled her grandmother. '*Grandmère* called me in a complete state after her visit. Apparently, you made quite an impression.'

Daniel busied himself with the coffee preparation. 'Your grandmother is lovely.'

'She is. She is very astute, too. She's convinced you're either a fortune hunter, a criminal, or hopelessly in love with my sister. Possibly all three.'

'And what do you think?' Daniel asked, fighting a smile.

'From all accounts, I think you're probably too sophisticated for a woman who's spent her entire life in Duckinwilla Creek, and I think my sister is too trusting for her own good.'

Daniel felt a flash of irritation. 'You underestimate Amelia.'

'Do I?' Charlotte leaned back in her chair. 'Because from where I'm sitting, it looks like she's playing house with a man she barely knows, in a situation that benefits you considerably more than it benefits her.'

'She had a two-bedroom house. I needed accommodation. It's a practical arrangement.'

'Is it? And the way you say her name suggests considerably more than practical interest.'

Daniel set a coffee cup in front of her with perhaps more force than necessary. 'What exactly are you suggesting?'

'I'm suggesting that my sister has a history of falling for strays,' Charlotte said bluntly. 'Wounded birds, stray cats, and now apparently charming, homeless Frenchmen with mysterious research projects. She sees the best in everyone, which is lovely in theory but problematic in practice. I've noticed her behaviour since your arrival.'

'I'm not a stray.'

'Aren't you?' Charlotte sipped her coffee, watching him over the rim. 'Temporary visitor, vague about your background, taking advantage of her generous nature? *Grandmère* has done her research.'

'I pay rent. I contribute to household

expenses. I'm hardly taking advantage.'

'Financially, perhaps not. But emotionally?' Charlotte shrugged. 'We've all noticed Amelia has been different since she moved out. Happier, but also... unsettled. Like she's waiting for something.'

Daniel felt something twist in his chest at the accuracy of that observation. He'd noticed it too—the way Amelia seemed to light up when he returned from his day at Henderson vineyard, the way she'd started cooking dinner in time for him to join her, the increasing depth of their conversations that stretched late into the evening. He knew her already, and he knew that she was happier away from her family. He understood that; the same reason he'd left the family business and gone to work for the company that acquired vineyards across the world. And then last night…

'Perhaps she's simply adjusting to living away from home,' he suggested.

'Perhaps. Or perhaps she's developing feelings for someone who's going to disappear back to France without a backward glance.'

The accusation hit closer to home than

Daniel cared to admit. 'You don't know what my intentions are.'

'Neither does she, and that's the problem.' Charlotte set down her cup and leaned forward. 'Look, I like you. You're clearly intelligent, you make excellent coffee, and you managed to hold your own with *Grandmère*, which is no small feat. But Amelia has spent her entire life taking care of other people—her students, her family, her friends. She deserves someone who's going to take care of her for a change, not someone who's going to add to her collection of good deeds.'

Daniel was saved from responding by the sound of the front door opening.

'Charlotte?' Amelia's voice carried down the hallway.

'In here,' Charlotte called back. 'Having a lovely chat with your housemate.'

Amelia appeared in the kitchen doorway; her cheeks flushed from the heat, and her blue hair escaping from its ponytail in the way that made Daniel smile. She looked between him and Charlotte warily.

'Charlotte. Why aren't you at school?'

'I had an appointment in town. I thought you didn't work today.'

'I do and forgot one of my folders.' Amelia folded her arms and glanced at him. 'How long have you been interrogating Daniel?'

'We've been having a perfectly civilised conversation,' Charlotte replied. 'Haven't we, Daniel?'

'We have.'

'That's a diplomatic way of putting it,' Amelia said, shooting her sister a warning look. 'I hope *Grandmere's* clone hasn't been giving you the third degree.'

'Just getting to know each other,' Charlotte said innocently. 'Weren't we, Daniel?'

'Yes, we were.' He looked from one sister to the other.

'I'm perfectly capable of taking care of myself, Charlotte.'

Something in Amelia's tone made Daniel's chest tighten.

Her sister nodded. 'Of course, you are. But there's no harm in being cautious, is there? After all, you don't really know very much about Daniel's background. His work, his plans...'

'Charlotte! Don't be rude.'

'Well, do you? For instance, how long is this project supposed to last?'

Both women looked at Daniel, waiting for an answer he couldn't give without revealing more than he could share.

'Research timelines are flexible.'

'Who are you working for?'

Sweat prickled at the back of his neck. He couldn't mention the Henderson acquisition; Amelia thought he was working for his family. 'I'm afraid I can't discuss the specifics. Confidentiality agreements, you understand.'

'Of course,' Charlotte said smoothly.

Doubt rose in Amelia's expression. A realisation that, for all their cosy chats at night, she really didn't know very much about what he actually did all day.

'Well,' Charlotte said, 'I should be getting back to school.'

She kissed Amelia goodbye and nodded politely to Daniel as she left.

'I apologise for my family again,' Amelia said, her tone was strained.

'It's okay. They just care about you.'

'Do you want to change your mind about lunch at *Grandmère*'s on Sunday? It will just be the same but worse.'

Daniel couldn't help himself. For all her brash confidence, he already knew that Amelia doubted herself. He walked over and put his hands on her shoulders.

'Hey, you, cheer up. I've dealt with a lot worse than that in my life.'

She looked up at him, and he was surprised to see tears misting her eyes. 'We're going to Sunday lunch and we're going to deal with your family. I don't like seeing you unhappy.'

He leaned down and brushed his lips over her cheek.

Before Amelia could respond, Daniel picked up his keys and headed for his car. 'Don't cook. I'll bring dinner home tonight.' He grinned at the domesticity of his comment.

Chapter 8

The front door closed with a soft click, and Amelia stood in the hallway, her cheek still tingling where Daniel's lips had touched.

Don't cook. I'll bring dinner home.

The word left a warm feeling in her chest. *Home.*

She touched her cheek; the gentle pressure of Daniel's mouth had been sweet. A reminder of the night they'd shared. Only a few weeks of sharing a house, and now he was talking about facing her family's interrogation like it was nothing.

I've dealt with a lot worse than that in my life.

What did that mean? Daniel never talked about his family—apart from the fact that his *Grandmère* was the same as hers, and that the family had a vineyard. She'd assumed it was just his way—some people were naturally private. But the way he'd said it, with something harder underneath his usual calm, made her wonder what he was not saying

Charlotte's and *Grandmere's* warnings crept

back in, but Amelia pushed them away. They'd managed to get out of the dreaded Sunday lunch until now, but she knew they wouldn't be able to again. Just because Daniel didn't talk about his family didn't mean he was hiding anything terrible. Maybe his family were the difficult ones. Maybe he'd learned early that sharing too much only led to disappointment.

Amelia pressed her back against the kitchen counter. A month. Had it really only been such a short time since Daniel moved in? It felt like longer, like they'd been living together for months.

But last night. Last night had changed everything.

Then she'd come back from the pre-school to collect a folder and had surprised Charlotte there giving Daniel the third degree.

When Charlotte had left and Daniel was about to leave, he hesitated and turned around like he'd forgotten something important.

Then he'd leaned in, quick and warm, and pressed his lips to her cheek. Right there, just below her ear, where her skin was sensitive.

'Don't cook. I'll bring dinner home tonight,'

he'd said, voice soft in that way that made her stomach flip.

He'd pulled back, smiled that slow smile of his, and walked out the door like he hadn't just turned her entire world sideways.

She'd stood there for ten minutes after his car disappeared, touching her cheek like some lovesick teenager.

She wandered back to the kitchen, still feeling the ghost of his touch. The coffee mugs from this morning sat in the sink. Such a small thing, but it felt significant somehow. Evidence of their morning routine, proof that this thing between them was real and growing.

Her phone buzzed. A photo from Daniel at the Thai place two doors down from the General Store, with the caption: **green curry or pad Thai**?

She smiled, typing back: **surprise me.**

Three dots appeared immediately, then: **I seem to be good at that.**

Heat crept up her neck. Yes, he was definitely good at surprises. Good at making her feel steady and off-balance all at once. Good at showing up exactly when she needed someone in her corner.

She was dreading the inevitable Sunday lunch. Mum would ask pointed questions about his job and his family. Dad would grunt disapproval into his beer. *Grandmère* would watch his every word like she was gathering evidence for a court case.

But Daniel would go. He'd looked her straight in the eye and promised to deal with whatever her family threw at them.

Amelia pressed her back against the counter, grinning at nothing. After such a short time of knowing him, she was already thinking in terms of *we* instead of *me*.

Maybe Charlotte was right about one thing; she was falling fast. But looking around the kitchen, seeing Daniel's jacket draped over the back of her chair and his coffee mug waiting to be washed, she couldn't bring herself to care about how short a time it was.

Some things were worth the risk.

Chapter 9

Daniel stood in the pre-dawn darkness of the cottage kitchen, laptop open on the table, staring at the email he'd drafted and deleted six times. Charlotte's interrogation yesterday had cut into his comfort zone. 'You don't really know very much about Daniel's background,' she'd said to Amelia, and she'd been absolutely right. Outside, the first hints of light touched the jacaranda tree, but sleep had eluded him entirely.

He and Amelia had shared the Thai takeaway, and laughed before they'd sat close on the sofa and watched another movie. It had ended late, and they'd gone to her bed and he'd not done the work he was supposed to.

So now he was deciding what to do.

Dear Jean,

I regret to inform you that I will be resigning from my position with Langlois Wine Consortium, effective immediately...

He deleted the words again and pushed the laptop away with a frustrated sigh. Charlotte's pointed questions had forced him to confront what he'd been avoiding: he was living a lie, and the woman he was falling in love with was defending a version of him that didn't exist. The coffee maker gurgled to life—he'd set it on auto last night, a small domestic ritual that would have amused his colleagues in Paris. Daniel Dupont, the man who'd closed deals in three countries and never stayed anywhere longer than his company required, setting coffee timers like a suburban husband.

His phone buzzed. Another message from Marcus: **Board meeting moved to 9 AM Paris time. They want the Henderson update. What do I tell them?**

What indeed? That he'd spent a month falling in love instead of closing a deal? That Mrs Henderson had seen right through his corporate charm and demanded watertight ethical guarantees his company would never provide? That he'd discovered he no longer had the stomach for treating family businesses like acquisitions to be stripped down for parts?

Daniel opened his laptop again and pulled up his employment contract. Five years with Langlois. Excellent salary, performance bonuses, international travel, fast track to partnership. Everything he'd wanted when he'd left Lyon and his father's disappointed expectations behind last year.

"You're throwing away your heritage for what? Corporate games in Paris?" His father's words still stung. The Dupont vineyard had been struggling, needed fresh ideas and investment, but Daniel had seen only limitations. Small family operation, traditional methods, the same conversations with the same neighbours about the same problems year after year.

Now, sitting in a kitchen that felt like home, those limitations felt different. Like roots instead of restrictions.

But was he romanticising everything because he was in love? A month ago, he'd been Daniel Dupont, rising star of international agricultural acquisition. Now he was considering throwing away his career for... what? A consulting business that didn't exist yet? The hope that a woman who'd known him for less than a month might want to build a life with him?

The rational part of his mind—the part that had negotiated million-euro deals—laid out the facts with brutal clarity; he had no clients for his hypothetical consulting firm.

His savings would last maybe six months in Australia.

His visa expired in less than five months.

Amelia had a life here, a job she loved, a family who needed her.

He was asking her to take a massive risk on someone who'd already proven he was willing to lie when convenient.

His phone rang. Jean Langlois.

'Dupont.' Daniel stepped onto the back patio, not wanting to wake Amelia.

'You missed the board meeting,' Jean's voice was ice-cold. 'Marcel asked specifically about the Henderson timeline, and I had nothing to tell him.'

'I'm still negotiating—'

'No, you're not. You're stalling. Marcus pulled your travel records. You haven't been to see Henderson in four days. What the hell are you doing over there?'

Daniel leaned against the patio railing, watching the sun creep over the cane fields. 'I'm reassessing the viability of the acquisition.'

'Reassessing?' Jean's laugh held disbelief.

'It's a technology purchase, not a philosophical debate. Close the property deal, buy the patents, license the software, and implement across our operations. It's not complicated.'

'Mrs Henderson isn't motivated by financial considerations. Her husband's technology represents his life's work. She wants assurance that it won't disappear into corporate research and development without him being acknowledged.'

'Then give her those assurances. Sign whatever agreements she wants. Promise her a memorial plaque if necessary. But close this deal.'

'It's not that simple—'

'It is exactly that simple,' Jean interrupted. 'You have one day to finalise this acquisition, or I'm sending Marcus over there to handle it. And if that happens, your position in the company becomes considerably less secure.'

The casual dismissal of Eleanor Henderson's concerns crystallised something Daniel had been trying not to acknowledge. 'You're planning to buy the technology and then ignore her conditions.'

'We're planning to maximise shareholder value, which is our job. Her feelings about her dead husband's legacy are not our concern.'

'They should be.'

The silence stretched long enough that Daniel wondered if the call had dropped.

'I beg your pardon?' Jean's voice was dangerously quiet.

'I said they should be our concern. Harold Henderson spent thirty years developing sustainable agricultural solutions. His widow deserves better than corporate doublespeak designed to placate her while we strip-mine his life's work.'

'Jesus Christ, Dupont. What's happened to you over there? Last year, you were complaining that family operations were too sentimental about intellectual property. Now you sound like some bleeding-heart activist.'

Last year. Had it really been such a short time since he'd seen family businesses as inefficient obstacles to corporate expansion? Since he'd measured success purely in acquisition targets and profit margins?

'Maybe I was wrong last year,' Daniel said

quietly.

Another long pause. 'Are you resigning?'

The question hung in the air like a challenge. Daniel thought about his apartment in Paris, pristine and expensive and utterly impersonal. About the partnership track he'd worked towards for five years. About the respect of colleagues who measured worth in deal closures and advancement speed.

Then he thought about Amelia's laugh when she told terrible jokes, about the way she'd defended him to her family even when he didn't deserve it, about the possibility of building something meaningful instead of just profitable. About the nights he'd spent in her bed.

'I don't know,' he said, and realised it was the first completely honest thing he'd said in the conversation.

'Well, figure it out. You have twenty-four hours to either close the Henderson deal or submit your resignation. We're not paying your salary to have an identity crisis on the other side of the world.'

The call ended, leaving Daniel alone with the sunrise and a decision that could reshape his entire life.

He went back inside to find Amelia in the kitchen, hair twisted up in a messy bun, wearing a faded T-shirt over her pyjama shorts. The sight of her, mussed hair and comfortable in her old clothes, tightened his chest with longing.

'Everything okay?'

'Couldn't sleep.' He poured coffee into two mugs, grateful for the familiar ritual. 'Work stuff.' He handed her a mug, their fingers brushing in a contact that somehow steadied him. 'Amelia, can I ask you something?'

'Of course.'

'When you decided to move out of your family's house, were you sure it was the right choice? Or did you just... leap and hope you'd figure out the landing?'

She considered this, sipping her coffee thoughtfully. 'Leap and hope, mostly. Why?'

'I'm facing a similar decision. About my job, about staying in Australia, about... us.' He met her eyes. 'And I'm terrified I'm about to make the wrong choice for all the right reasons.'

'What would be the wrong choice?'

'Giving up a career I've worked towards for

over a year to start over in a country I've lived in for a month, with a business plan that exists mostly in my head, because I've fallen in love with someone who deserves better than a man having a quarter-life crisis.'

Amelia set down her mug and moved closer, close enough that he could smell her lemon shampoo.

'Daniel,' she said softly, 'what would be the right choice?'

He thought about Jean's casual dismissal of Eleanor Henderson's concerns, about the apartment in Paris that felt like a hotel room, about the partnership track that led to more of the same work he was beginning to hate.

Then he thought about the consulting firm he could build, helping farmers implement sustainable technologies instead of selling their properties to corporations. About morning coffee conversations and terrible jokes and the possibility of belonging somewhere instead of just passing through.

'I don't know,' he said honestly. 'But I think I'm ready to find out.'

Amelia smiled, the expression lighting up

her entire face. 'Then that's not a leap, Daniel. That's just the next step.'

Daniel realised she was right. He wasn't throwing away his career on a whim—he was choosing to build something better, something of his own, with someone worth the risk.

He stared at her, hoping Amelia would support the crazy decision he knew he was going to make.

'Is everything okay at home? Your family?' she asked with a frown.

'Something like that. Everything's fine.'

'Are you sure?'

'Yes, I have some paperwork to do.' It wasn't exactly a lie, but he felt bad. He couldn't meet her eyes. 'Nothing important.'

'Hey.' She touched his arm, and his nerves zinged beneath her gentle fingers. 'What's wrong? You look worried.'

'Nothing's wrong.'

'You're a terrible liar.'

Her phone buzzed on the table.

Chapter 10

'Who messages this early?' Amelia said with a frown, crossing to the table and picking up her phone 'Oh, it's Lisette. She wants to know if I'm awake. Something must be wrong.' She put her hand on his arm. 'Stay there, and we'll continue our conversation in a moment.'

Daniel couldn't hear Lisette's side of the conversation, but he could get the gist of it from Amelia's responses and body language. Her initial wariness gave way to concern, then what looked like frustration.

'No, Lisette, you don't understand,' Amelia said, turning away from Daniel. 'He's not like that. He's decent and honest, and just because he doesn't broadcast every detail of his life doesn't mean he's hiding something sinister.'

The words hit Daniel hard. Decent and honest. He stared at Amelia's back as she defended him. His chest surged with guilt.

'I know you're trying to protect me,' Amelia continued, turning around to hold his gaze, 'but I'm not some naive country girl who can't tell the difference between charm and a genuine guy.

Daniel is... he's good, Lisette. Really good. And I am not going to let the family interfere.'

She trusted him. Despite all her family's interference, despite the half-truths she was unaware of, she had looked at their time together and decided he was worth defending.

The realisation that he was about to prove her completely wrong had his stomach churning.

'I have to go,' Amelia said into the phone. 'I'll talk to you later.'

She hung up and looked at him, her cheeks flushed.

'Sorry about that. Lisette is... she means well, but she can be overprotective.'

'What did she want?' Daniel asked, though he suspected he already knew.

'She's worried I'm being too trusting. She thinks I don't know enough about your background to be sharing a house with you.' Amelia's smile was soft but held frustration. 'I told her she was wrong. I told her I trust you.'

The simple statement hit like an accusation. Daniel felt every careful lie he'd told, every omission, crystallise into pressure on his chest.

'Amelia—'

'I should get ready for school,' she interrupted. 'I've got an early start this morning.'

She was already moving towards the hallway when Daniel's laptop chimed with an incoming email. He glanced at the screen automatically and felt his stomach drop. The message was from Marcus, with a subject line that read 'Henderson Agricultural Solutions - Final Contract Terms'.

'*Merde*,' he muttered, immediately moving to close the laptop, but it was too late. All his morning's agonising about honesty and deception, all the soul-searching Charlotte's visit had triggered—and now this. The decision was being made for him.

Amelia had frozen in the kitchen doorway. She was staring at his laptop screen with an expression Daniel couldn't quite read.

'Henderson Vineyard Solutions,' she said slowly. 'That was Mr Henderson's company. And Mrs Henderson, who owns this house.'

Daniel felt every muscle in his body tense. 'Amelia—'

'You knew Mrs Henderson already.' It wasn't a question. 'That's why you're here. Not for research. For her company.'

He watched as the pieces fell into place for her. Daniel saw the exact moment Amelia realised the scope of his deception.

'You're here to buy her company,' Amelia continued, her voice deadly quiet. 'You're here on business, not research. Corporate acquisition, not agricultural study.'

'It's more complicated than that—'

'Is it?' Amelia strode towards the laptop, her eyes scanning the email on the screen. 'Final contract terms. Acquisition timeline. How long have you been lying to me, Daniel?'

'I haven't been lying. I've just not told you everything.'

The words sounded pathetic even to his own ears. Amelia looked at him with an expression he'd never seen before—not anger, not hurt, but a cold assessment that made his skin crawl

'Acquisition,' she said. 'Right. So when I asked about your research, and you talked about soil analysis and crop management, that was a lie?'

'The technology Mr Henderson developed does involve soil analysis—'

'Don't.' The single word cut through his explanation like a blade. 'Don't make this worse by trying to justify it with technicalities.'

Daniel felt the conversation spiralling beyond his control, could see the growing distance in Amelia's eyes even as she stood three feet away from him. 'Amelia, please. Let me explain.'

'Explain what? How you've been using me? How you've been living in my house, eating meals I cooked, letting me defend you to my family, all while lying about who you are and why you're here? They were right. I am a gullible fool.'

'That's not—I never used you. This arrangement, our... whatever this is between us, it has nothing to do with my work.'

'Doesn't it?' Amelia's laugh was sharp, humourless. 'Convenient local accommodation while you butter up Mrs Henderson. Someone to vouch for your character, maybe? The sweet local girl who can assure suspicious elderly ladies that you're trustworthy?'

'You know that's not true. I met her before I knew you were in this house.'

'Do I? Because three minutes ago I told my sister—my astute sister, one of my astute family, that you were decent and honest, and it turns out I don't know anything about you at all.'

Desperation clawed at his chest. 'Let me explain. I know it's been a short time, but you know me. You know me. This—' he gestured between them '—what we have, it's real. It has nothing to do with business.'

'What we have,' Amelia said slowly, 'is me being an idiot. Me trusting someone who's been lying to me from the moment we met.'

'I never lied—'

'Omission is still deception, Daniel. Letting me believe something you know isn't true is still lying.' Her voice was getting quieter, more controlled, which was worse than if she'd been shouting. 'How long were you planning to keep this up? Until you closed your deal? Until you flew back to France? Were you ever going to tell me the truth?'

The honest answer was that he didn't know. He stared at her.

'I see,' Amelia said. She turned to the door. 'I think you should find somewhere else to stay.

Now.'

The words hit him like a physical blow. 'Amelia, please—'

'I'm going to work,' she continued as if he hadn't spoken. 'I'd appreciate it if you could be gone by the time I'm home.'

'Where am I supposed to go?'

'I don't know. Maybe ask Mrs Henderson if she has a spare room. I'm sure she'd be delighted to accommodate such an honest, straightforward house guest.' Her eyes widened. 'Or doesn't she know what you're after either?'

The sarcasm in her voice was worse than anger would have been. Daniel watched her walk towards the hallway, wanting to follow her, wanting to explain, wanting to fix this somehow. But every word he could think of was inadequate.

'Amelia,' he called, desperation making his voice rough. 'I'm sorry. I never meant for this to happen.'

She paused at the door, her hand on the handle, but didn't turn around.

'The really tragic thing,' she said quietly, 'is that I believe you. I don't think you meant for any of this to happen. I don't think you planned to hurt me. But you did it anyway, and that somehow makes it worse.'

The bedroom door closed behind her with a quiet finality.

Daniel stood alone in the kitchen, his eyes closed, breathing deeply. Ten minutes after she walked through, dressed for school, and drove off, his laptop chimed again with another email from Marcus, probably wondering about timeline updates and contract negotiations. The corporate world that had defined him for the past year was still there demanding his attention.

But for the first time since he'd started working for them, Daniel couldn't bring himself to care about quarterly reports and profit margins. All he could think about was the way Amelia had said his name when she defended him to her sister, the trust in her voice when she called him decent and honest, the quiet devastation in her eyes when she realised how wrong she'd been.

He'd spent the past month falling in love with a woman who deserved honesty, and he'd repaid her trust with deception. Daniel finally understood what he'd done. And he knew how much he cared about her.

And he also knew that understanding it now was a month too late.

Chapter 11

Daniel was waiting when his phone rang later that morning.

'Dupont.' Jean Langlois, the head of operations and a man who measured success in quarterly reports and margin improvements. 'What's the deal?'

Daniel left his laptop on the kitchen table, stepped out onto the front porch, keeping his voice low. 'Good afternoon, Jean. I assume this is about the Henderson acquisition.'

'Do we have a signature on the contract?'

'No.'

'I accept your resignation.'

The call disconnected, and Daniel closed his eyes.

***

Amelia had barely functioned at school and had rushed off as soon as the last child had been picked up just after three.

As she drove home, exhaustion weighed on her like a physical thing. She'd managed to block

Daniel from her mind for some of the day. Work had given her something to focus on besides the hollow ache in her chest. On the way home, she rehearsed the conversation she would have with the family, dismissing Daniel with a laugh and saying, 'Oh, Daniel? He had to go back to France. I had you all convinced there was something between us, didn't I?' She would laugh and pull it off. She had to, because she couldn't stand to lose face with them all.

But now, turning into her driveway, she froze. His rental car was still there.

Her legs trembled as she strode towards the house, her calm beginning to crack. Daniel was supposed to be gone. She was supposed to reclaim her independence today, return to the simple life she'd been building before a charming Frenchman had complicated everything with his excellent coffee and devastating smile.

The sound of footsteps in the hallway made her feel ill as she walked through the door. She would never, ever be gullible again. She would never trust again.

He appeared in the doorway of the kitchen,

and for a moment, Amelia forgot to breathe. Even after a month, his good looks hit her anew. If anything, familiarity had only made her more aware of the details that made him so devastatingly gorgeous. The way his dark hair fell across his forehead when he was concentrating, how his eyes seemed to shift from brown to gold depending on his mood, the elegant way he moved his hands when he was trying to find the right words in English. Today, those hands were gripping the doorframe as if he needed the support, and there were lines around his eyes.

'I know you asked me to leave,' he said before she could speak. 'But I couldn't. Not like this. Not with you thinking...' He trailed off, running a hand through his hair in the gesture she'd learned meant he was struggling with something.

'Thinking what?' Amelia asked, proud of how steady her voice sounded despite the way her heart was hammering against her ribs.

'Thinking that everything between us was a lie.'

She wanted to push past him, to maintain the

cold anger that had kept her focused all day. But there was something raw in his voice, a vulnerability she'd never heard before, that made her pause.

'Wasn't it?' she asked quietly.

'No.' The word came out fierce, almost angry. 'What happened between us, what's been happening... that was never part of any business plan. That was never supposed to happen at all.'

Despite herself, Amelia's resolve wavered. 'But you did lie about why you're here.'

'Yes.' He didn't try to soften it or explain it away, which somehow made the admission worse and better at the same time. 'I lied about my work, about my timeline, about why I'm in Australia. But I never lied about...' He gestured helplessly between them. 'About this. About how I feel when you laugh at your own terrible jokes, or the way you sing in the shower, or how you make everything feel less complicated just by being yourself.'

Tears pricked at the back of her eyes, and she forced them away. 'That doesn't change what you did.'

'I know. And I know I have no right to ask

for forgiveness, but I'm asking anyway. Not for the business deception—I understand if you can't forgive that. But for the chance to explain. To tell you the truth, all of it, and let you decide if there's anything worth salvaging.'

She should have said no. Every instinct honed by twenty-two years of being the responsible daughter told her to walk away from the man who'd deceived her. But there was something in Daniel's eyes—a desperation that matched the hollow ache in her own chest—that made her nod instead.

'All right,' she said. 'You can explain. But I'm making my coffee, and if you so much as attempt to help or touch me, this conversation is over.'

Relief flooded his features so completely that Amelia had to look away.

'Of course. Whatever you want.'

She pushed past him, aware of the way he stepped aside to avoid any accidental touch. The kitchen looked exactly as she'd left it this morning.

'Talk,' she said curtly, as she turned on the coffee machine, and then set a pan on the gas to begin cooking dinner. Not that she was hungry; she needed to keep her mind on something other than Daniel still in her kitchen. 'Start with who you really are and why you're here.'

Daniel settled at the kitchen table, carefully positioning himself where she could see him while she cooked. 'My name is Daniel Dupont, and I work for Langlois Wine Consortium. We're a Paris-based company that specialises in innovative farming solutions for French vineyards.'

Amelia pushed a pod into the machine and positioned her cup, not trusting herself to look at him directly. 'And Mrs Henderson?'

'Her late husband developed a unique soil analysis system that could revolutionise grape growing. We—or the company—want to buy the technology and implement it commercially.'

'So, you came here to charm a lonely widow into selling her husband's life's work.' The words came out harsher than she'd intended, but Amelia didn't take them back.

'Initially, yes. That was the plan.' Daniel's voice was quiet, carefully controlled. 'Mrs Henderson has refused other offers because she doesn't trust that the technology will be used responsibly. My job was to convince her otherwise.'

'And how's that working out for you?'

'Not well. She's... perceptive. She asks difficult questions about implementation. She wants guarantees that his technology won't disappear into corporate research indefinitely.'

Despite herself, she nodded in approval. Eleanor Henderson had always been smart, not the kind of woman to be easily manipulated by corporate charm. 'Good for her.'

The machine hissed, and hot coffee overflowed from the cup, scalding Amelia's hand as she gripped the countertop beside the machine

'Are you all right?' Daniel was on his feet immediately, moving towards her before remembering he wasn't supposed to touch her.

'I'm fine,' Amelia said automatically, running cold water on her fingers. 'What else did she say?'

'She found it interesting that you were happy to share the house with me. She doesn't know...' Daniel trailed off, seemingly unsure how to finish the sentence.

'Know what? That you've been using me as a character reference? Local girl vouches for mysterious Frenchman's trustworthiness?'

'That I've fallen in love with you.'

Amelia stared at Daniel, her heart racing.

'You can't say that,' she whispered.

'Why not? It's true.'

'Because you lied to me for a whole month. Because you're here on business and I'm just... I'm just the convenient local accommodation. Because—'

The smoke alarm's ear-splitting shriek cut through her words. Amelia spun around to see flames licking up from the frying pan she'd forgotten she'd put on the stove, the oil she'd been heating now burning with enthusiastic orange tongues.

'*Merde*,' Daniel swore, lunging for the stove controls while Amelia grabbed for the fire extinguisher under the sink. They collided in the middle of the kitchen, Daniel's arms coming around her to steady them both as she fumbled with the extinguisher pin.

'Turn off the gas,' she said, surprised by how

calm her voice sounded.

'Already done. Stand back.'

She aimed the extinguisher at the pan while Daniel opened windows and waved at the smoke alarm with a tea towel. The fire died with a pathetic hiss, leaving behind the acrid smell of burnt oil. They stood in the smoke-filled kitchen, staring at each other.

'Well,' Amelia said finally, 'that's one way to avoid an awkward conversation.'

Daniel laughed—a short, surprised sound that seemed to surprise him as much as it did her. 'Are you hurt?'

'Just my pride.' She looked down at the extinguisher in her hands, then at the ruined pan, then at Daniel standing three feet away with his hair mussed from waving the tea towel and his shirt rumpled. Through the lingering smoke, she stared at him; there was something gentle in the way he looked at her. 'I can't believe I nearly burned down my own kitchen.'

'Our kitchen,' Daniel said quietly.

Amelia set down the fire extinguisher. His face was drawn, exhaustion evident in the shadows under his eyes and the way he held his shoulders.

'Daniel,' she began, not sure what she intended to say.

'I know I don't deserve another chance,' he interrupted. 'I know I've broken your trust in a way that might be irreparable. But I need you to know that what I said is true. I never meant for this to happen. I never meant to fall in love with you. But I did, and now I can't imagine going back to a life I without you in it.'

'I'm sorry,' she whispered, and she wasn't sure if she was apologising for the fire, for her anger, or for the way her heart was racing despite everything he'd done.

'No, I'm sorry.' He took a step closer, then stopped, as if unsure whether he was allowed. 'I should have told you the truth from the beginning. I should have—'

'Stay with me,' she said. 'Just... for a while. We can figure out the rest later.'

They made two coffees—and took them to her bedroom to get away from the smoke-smelling kitchen. With their backs against the bedhead, they talked about everything. Daniel told her about his childhood in Lyon, about the pressure from his family to stay in the family vineyard, but his determination to prove his independence.

'Well, I certainly understand that,' she said.

He said he'd never planned on staying in one place long enough to form any attachments. Amelia shared stories she rarely told anyone, small pieces of her past that felt safe enough to give away.

As the minutes passed, they moved lower on the bed, still talking, still fully clothed. Daniel lay on his side facing her, head propped on his hand, and she mirrored his position. The space between them was small enough that their knees touched, and she could see the gold flecks in his brown eyes.

'What are you thinking about?' he asked when she was quiet for a while.

'How different you look up close.'

'Different how?'

She studied his face—the strong line of his nose, the fullness of his bottom lip, the way his eyes crinkled slightly at the corners when he smiled. 'Less like someone who's about to leave.'

'I don't want to leave,' he said quietly. 'That's what scared me.'

The simple honesty of his words made her chest tighten. She reached out, tracing the line of his jaw with one finger. He caught her hand, pressing it flat against his cheek.

'Amelia.'

'Yes?'

'I know you're scared. I'm scared too. But can we just... stay together? Without thinking about tomorrow? Maybe trust that the future works out. Give us a chance?'

She nodded, and he pulled her closer until her head was tucked under his chin and his heart beat against her cheek. His arms came around her, secure and warm, and for the first time in longer than she could remember, she was content.

She must have slept all night because the next thing she knew, it was seven a.m. and her alarm was buzzing. Daniel was asleep, his breathing deep and even, one arm still wrapped around her. In sleep, he looked younger, dark lashes fanned against his cheeks, that perpetual slight furrow between his brows finally smoothed away.

She should leave, she thought. Slip out of her bed and give them both space to think about what had happened, pretend this was just a moment of weakness brought on by a kitchen fire.

When was the last time someone had held her like this? When was the last time she'd wanted them to?

His eyes opened slowly, immediately finding hers. For a moment, neither of them moved, both aware that whatever had happened, it was a fragile peace.

'Hi,' he said softly.

'Hi.'

'Any regrets?'

She considered lying, but something in his expression—hopeful and vulnerable and trying so hard to appear casual—stopped her. 'No,' she said, and meant it. 'You?'

'Not even close. Amelia?'

'Yes?'

'Before we had words, I told my boss I wasn't doing it. I no longer have a job with them.'

'How do you feel about that?

He held her eyes with his. 'Happy, and I know I have made the right decision.'

They lay there for a while longer, not talking, just existing in this strange new space they'd created. Eventually, life intruded—the smoke smell from the kitchen needed to be dealt with, and she had to get ready for work.

But as Daniel finally slipped out of her bed and padded towards the bathroom, Amelia knew something had changed between them. They'd crossed a line, and there was no going back.

The question now was whether they'd both survive what came next.

Chapter 12

Daniel had been living in the house with Amelia for over a month now, but he'd never seen *Grandmère* and Papa's estate until *Grandmère* had issued an ultimatum for Sunday dinner.

'*Plus d'excuses*,' *Grandmère* had decreed when she called the day after the fire.

'Yes, *Grandmère*. No more excuses, we'll be there.' Daniel had smiled when Amelia assured her grandmother, and rolled her eyes.

The sprawling homestead just outside Duckinwilla was nothing like what he'd expected—acres of rolling paddocks, ancient gum trees, and a beautiful house in a new estate.

'You'll love *Grandmère*'s roast lamb,' Amelia said during the drive over, her knuckles white on the steering wheel. 'And Dad's... well, he's having some good days and some not-so-good days lately. Just go with whatever he says, all right?'

Daniel had nodded, though privately he'd wondered what exactly constituted a "not-so-good day" for Hugo Johnson.

Now, watching the family dinner unfold from his position across from Amelia at the long dining table in *Grandmère*'s formal dining room, he was beginning to understand.

The table could easily seat twenty, and today it was hosting the extended Johnson family—Amelia's parents, Hugo and Ellen, her siblings Julien, with his wife Emily, Charlotte and her husband, Greg, Guy with his new wife, Elena, and Oliver with his partner, Sarah. Lisette hadn't come home for lunch, even though her presence had been requested with an email.

'So, Daniel,' Hugo said, cutting into his lamb. 'Amelia tells me you're researching agricultural methods. We've been trying some new irrigation techniques on the farm.' He paused, fork halfway to his mouth, a slight frown creasing his brow. 'When did we start that? Last season?'

'Two seasons ago, Dad,' Oliver said gently from his position next to Sarah. 'Remember? You and Guy spent months planning the new drip system.'

'Right, yes. Of course.' Hugo's smile was quick. 'Time plays tricks, doesn't it? Especially when you've been farming as long as I have.'

Daniel exchanged a glance with Amelia, who was pushing food around her plate without actually eating. Her shoulders were rigid.

'Daniel's from Lyon originally,' *Grandmère* told the family, her sharp eyes moving between her granddaughter and the man she'd decided to approve of. 'It is a beautiful city.'

'*Merci*, Madame Dubois,' Daniel replied.

'Lyon!' Hugo's face lit up. 'Wonderful city. I took the family there in... well, when the children were young. We stayed near the Cathedral, didn't we, Ellen?'

'That was last year, love,' Ellen said quietly, reaching over to squeeze her husband's hand. 'We went to Lyon with your parents, and Greg and Charlotte.'

Daniel watched the expression that crossed Hugo's face—confusion, followed by a flash of something that might have been embarrassment, then the quick recovery smile again. But what struck him more was the way the entire family seemed to cope.

Except Amelia, she had gone very still.

'Right, yes. Last year.' Hugo cleared his

throat. 'Gets confusing, all these French cities. They're all so...' He trailed off, staring at his plate as if he'd forgotten what he was saying.

The silence stretched just long enough to become uncomfortable before Charlotte jumped in with a bright comment about her latest work project at the high school.

Daniel sat back fascinated by the family dynamic.

Amelia's *Grandmère* reminded him of his grandmother at home. She was the steady centre—calm, unflappable, with the kind of iron strength that held families together through crises. Julien had inherited his father's natural leadership and seemed to balance running the family's General Store with a close relationship with Emily, his wife. Charlotte was warm and practical, clearly used to dealing with difficult situations in her teaching career, and Daniel noticed she and Greg exchanged glances whenever someone mentioned the farm. Guy was quieter, more observant, but Daniel caught him looking concerned whenever his father struggled with a memory. Oliver had the easy confidence of someone who worked well with his hands, though Daniel noticed he was quicker than the others to cover awkward moments with practical suggestions about farm work.

And Amelia... Amelia was watching everything. She didn't miss a trick. Her eyes clouded every time her father seemed to lose the thread of conversation. She anticipated his needs before he voiced them, redirecting his words when he started to repeat himself,

She was exhausting herself trying to smooth the situation.

'So, Daniel,' Guy said, leaning back in his chair. 'What's the plan? Are you thinking of staying in Australia long-term, or is this just a temporary research stint?'

It was an innocent question, the kind any family might ask their daughter's... what was he, exactly? Housemate? Friend? Something undefined that had crossed several lines three mornings ago?

'I'm not entirely sure yet,' Daniel said carefully. 'It depends on several things.'

'Oh, how wonderfully vague,' Charlotte said, earning a smile from Greg. 'Spoken like a true researcher. Come on, give us something concrete. Six months? A year? Forever?'

Daniel felt heat rise in his cheeks. The truth was that his visa allowed him to stay for six months, and he'd been actively avoiding thinking about that deadline since the morning Amelia had fallen asleep in his arms.

'Charlotte,' Amelia warned, but her sister was clearly enjoying herself.

'What? I'm just trying to get a sense of the timeline. You know, for planning purposes. Family gatherings, holidays, whether we should start shopping for wedding venues—'

'Charlotte,' Amelia said again, more sharply this time.

'I'm only joking! Mostly.' Charlotte winked at Daniel. 'But seriously, it's nice to see Amelia with someone who doesn't bore her to tears. The last bloke she brought home spent the entire evening talking about different types of fertilisers.'

'That was a very educational evening,' Hugo said suddenly. 'Crop nutrition is fascinating. Did you know that cane requires different nutrient ratios depending on—' He stopped abruptly, looking around the table with the expression of someone who'd lost track of his thought mid-sentence.

The pause stretched.

'Different nutrient ratios depending on the growth stage,' Amelia finished gently. 'That's right, Dad.'

'Yes.' Hugo's relief was palpable. 'Exactly. Clever girl, my Amelia. Always was the brightest of the bunch.'

Daniel watched Amelia's face carefully. There was love there, and patience, but also worry. He recognised the look—it was the same expression his mother had worn during his grandfather's final years, when every conversation became a navigation exercise.

'*Grand-père* had dementia,' he said quietly to Amelia when the loud conversation around the table had moved on to safer topics. 'I remember how exhausting it was for *Maman*, always being vigilant.'

Amelia's eyes snapped to his, wide and slightly panicked. 'Dad doesn't have—we don't know that it's—'

'I'm not diagnosing,' Daniel said quickly. 'I'm just saying I understand why you look tired.'

For a moment, her carefully maintained composure cracked. 'He's seeing a specialist next week. It's probably just stress, or maybe his blood pressure. It could be lots of things.'

'Of course it could.' Daniel smiled at her. 'And whatever it is, your family will handle it. You're all very good at taking care of each other.'

'Amelia's the best at it,' Julien said, catching the tail end of their conversation. 'Always has been. Remember when I broke my ribs playing rugby and Mum was away at that CWA conference? Amelia was only thirteen, but she managed everything—hospital visits, helping me shower, even organising my school assignments so I wouldn't fall behind.'

'Amelia didn't organise his assignments,' Ellen said with a laugh. 'She supervised while he did them very, very slowly.'

'Same thing,' Julien grinned. 'Point is, our Amelia's always been the responsible one. Takes after Dad in that way—can't help but look after everyone else.'

Daniel glanced at Hugo, who was smiling

vaguely at his eldest son but seemed to have missed the compliment entirely. The older man was staring past Julien's shoulder with the unfocused expression Daniel recognised as confusion.

'Dad?' Amelia said gently. 'You alright?'

Hugo blinked, his gaze sharpening as it focused on his daughter. 'Of course, love. Just thinking about... about...' Another pause, longer this time. 'What were we talking about?'

The table went quiet. Daniel could feel the tension, the way everyone seemed to lean forward slightly, ready to help but unsure how. He noticed the partners—Emily, Greg, Elena, and Sarah—all looking uncertainly between the family members, clearly still learning how to deal with the situation.

'We were talking about how wonderful Amelia is,' *Grandmère* said smoothly. 'And how lucky Daniel is to have found her.' Her husband reached for her hand, but not before Daniel noticed the tears misting her eyes.

'Yes,' Hugo said, latching onto the familiar thread. 'Very lucky indeed. Though I should probably ask you about your intentions, shouldn't I?' He turned to Daniel with a sharp look that reminded Daniel exactly where Amelia had inherited her no-nonsense directness. 'Are you planning to marry my daughter?'

Charlotte choked on her wine. Guy's eyebrows shot towards his hairline. Ellen made a small sound that might have been suppressed laughter or horror. Even Papa looked up from his lamb with interest.

Amelia's cheeks were scarlet. 'Dad, for God's sake—'

'It's a reasonable question,' Hugo continued, apparently oblivious to the chaos he'd created. 'You're living together, aren't you? In my day, that meant something.'

Daniel felt every eye at the table turn to him. In the sudden silence, he could hear the tick of the mantel clock and the distant sound of a neighbour's lawnmower.

'Papa,' Amelia whispered, her mortification so complete it was almost painful to witness. 'Interrupt Dad. Please. Do something.'

But Hugo wasn't finished. 'I know I get confused sometimes,' he said, his voice taking on a quality Daniel hadn't heard before—rawer, more in the present. 'I know you all think I don't notice when I lose track of things. But I'm not stupid, and I'm not blind. This young man looks at you like you're his entire world, Amelia. And you've been happier these past weeks than I've seen you for a long time.'

Amelia blinked back tears as she held Daniel's eyes.

'Mr Johnson,' he said quietly, meeting the older man's gaze directly. 'I think your daughter is extraordinary. And if I'm lucky enough that she might consider a future with me, I promise you I'll spend every day trying to deserve her.'

It wasn't a proposal—it wasn't even close.

Hugo studied him for a long moment, then nodded slowly. 'Good answer.'

'Dad,' Amelia said, her voice thick with emotion.

'What? I like him. He speaks French properly, and he doesn't treat me like I'm made of glass like the rest of you are.' Hugo turned back to his dinner with the air of a man who'd accomplished something important. 'Now, who wants to slice the raspberry tart your *Grandmère* made? It looks magnificent.'

The conversation resumed, but Amelia remained quiet for the rest of the meal. When they finally said their goodbyes—a process that involved multiple rounds of hugs and promises to visit again soon—she was still subdued.

'I'm sorry,' she said as they drove home through the gathering dusk. 'About Dad's interrogation. He was the last one I expected to be so upfront. He doesn't usually... well, actually, he probably does usually ask questions like that. I just haven't brought anyone home in so long that I'd forgotten.'

'Don't apologise.' Daniel reached over to touch her hand where it rested on the gear stick. 'He loves you. They all do. It's obvious.'

'He embarrassed you.'

'He surprised me. There's a difference.' Daniel was quiet for a moment, watching the now familiar landscape pass 'Can I ask you something?'

'I suppose.'

'How long has he been having... episodes like that?'

Amelia's hands tightened on the steering wheel. 'It's not episodes. It's just... he gets confused sometimes. Forgets words or mixes up timelines. His doctor says it could be a lot of things. That's why he's referred him to a specialist.'

'But you're worried it's not.'

She was quiet for so long that Daniel thought she wasn't going to answer. 'Amelia,' he said gently, 'you know you can't stop this by managing everyone's reactions to it, right?'

'I can make it easier for him. I can make sure he doesn't feel embarrassed by his poor memory or his confusion. I can—'

'You can exhaust yourself trying to control things that are beyond your control.'

She pulled into their driveway and turned off the engine, but made no move to get out of the car. Daniel could see the tears trickling down her cheeks.

'Dad raised me to be responsible,' she said finally. 'To take care of people. How am I supposed to just watch him struggle and not do everything I can to help?'

Daniel unbuckled his seatbelt and turned to face her fully. 'You can help him. But you can't save him from getting older, and you can't save your family from the pain of watching him change. All you can do is love him through it.'

'How do you know that?' The question came out raw, almost accusatory.

'Because I tried to save my grandfather too. I researched every treatment, every medication, every alternative therapy. I drove myself crazy trying to find a way to give him back the man he'd been. And in the end, all I did was miss the man he still was.'

Amelia turned to look at him then, her eyes searching his face in the dim light. 'What changed?'

'My mother sat me down and told me that loving someone doesn't mean fixing them. It means being present with them, exactly as they are, for as long as you have.'

They sat in silence for a moment.

'I'm so scared,' she whispered.

'I know.'

'And I don't know how to stop trying to fix everything.'

'You don't have to stop. You just have to let other people help you.'

She laughed, the sound caught somewhere

between tears and genuine amusement. 'Pot, meet kettle.'

'Touché.' Daniel reached over to wipe a tear from her cheek with his thumb. 'We're both very good at carrying the world on our shoulders, aren't we?'

'Terrible habit.'

'The worst.' He leaned forward to rest his forehead against hers. 'Amelia?'

'Mmm?'

'Thank you for trusting me with this. With your family. I know it's not easy for you to let people see the difficult parts.'

She pulled back to look at him directly. 'Thank you for not running when my father asked if you were going to propose.'

Daniel felt heat rise in his cheeks again. 'About that...'

'Don't worry. I know you were just being polite. Family dinners make people say all sorts of things they don't mean.'

But that was the problem, Daniel realised as they finally made their way inside. He wasn't just being polite. Looking at Amelia across her family's lunch table, watching her handle her father's confusion with love, seeing the way her whole family adored and depended on the youngest child—somewhere in the middle of all that chaos, the idea of a future with her had struck him.

It had started feeling like something he desperately wanted.

And that terrified him almost as much as it thrilled him because wanting a future with Amelia would mean they would have to choose between France or Duckinwilla Creek.

Chapter 13

Amelia sighed when the toast popped up burnt, adding to the smoky smell that had lingered in the kitchen all week. In a way, it made her smile; the night of the fire had been the turning point in their relationship. She glanced at the clock as she put another piece of bread in the toaster.

Daniel had already left for his meeting with Mrs Henderson, and to make an offer to advise her, if she would trust him as a consultant. The cottage felt empty without him. She jumped when her phone buzzed in her pocket.

'Amelia?' Mum's voice crackled through the phone. 'Dr Mitchell wants to see the family this afternoon. Can you get away from work early?'

Amelia's stomach dropped. 'What did he say? Is Dad—'

'I don't know, love. The doctor wants to explain it properly to everyone together. Can you be at the clinic by three?'

She waited until the next piece of toast

popped up, looked at it, put it in the bin and headed to work.

Amelia was unusually impatient with the children as the day dragged. She texted Daniel: **Could be late. Not sure.**

By the time she reached the medical centre, the entire Johnson family had assembled in Dr Mitchell's waiting room. Charlotte hugged her as she walked in and gestured to her phone, where Lisette waited quietly on the FaceTime screen. Mum sat beside Dad, holding his hand, white knuckled. Julien paced near the window, and Guy flanked Oliver, who was bouncing his leg with the nervous habit he'd always had.

'Right,' Dr Mitchell said when he came into the waiting room. They were the only ones there. 'Thank you all for coming in. I know how difficult the wait has been for the family, but I have excellent news.'

Amelia swallowed, not daring to hope as Dad's attention was focused on Dr Mitchell.

'Hugo, your cognitive issues are entirely medication-related. Your blood pressure tablets are interacting with the new arthritis medication Dr Sanders prescribed. The combination was causing what we call cognitive clouding—confusion, memory lapses, difficulty finding words.'

Amelia's legs went weak with relief, and she collapsed onto one of the plastic chairs. 'So, it's not—he doesn't have—'

'No signs of dementia or Alzheimer's,' Dr Mitchell confirmed with a smile. 'We've adjusted the medication, and you should all see significant improvement within the next few days. Some people are simply more sensitive to drug interactions than others.'

'But he seemed so confused,' Charlotte said, voicing what they were all thinking. 'The way he lost track of conversations, forgot things that had just happened—'

'Classic signs of medication interaction in older adults,' the doctor explained. 'It's more common than you might think. The important thing is that it's completely reversible.'

Dad, who had been quiet until now, finally spoke up. 'So, I'm not losing my mind?'

'Definitely not losing your mind,' Dr Mitchell assured him. 'Though I suspect you've been worried about that possibility.'

'Terrified,' Dad admitted, squeezing Mum's hand.

The walk to their respective cars was filled with happy chat. Guy actually laughed—*laughed*—when Oliver suggested stopping for ice cream to celebrate. Charlotte immediately began planning a celebration family dinner for the weekend.

'We're going to *Grandmère* and Papa's before we come home,' Dad announced. 'To tell them the news. We'll see you back at the farm.'

Exuberance flooded through Amelia as Charlotte followed her home, and the boys caught up to them after they went to the store with Julien, who sent home three tubs of their favourite ice-creams. The worry she'd been carrying for weeks, the concentration, the exhausting responsibility of managing everyone else's fears—all of it lifted so suddenly she felt dizzy with happiness. The laughter at the farm that afternoon was cathartic for the whole family. When Amelia went to the pantry to get a container to take some leftover ice cream home to Daniel, she grinned as she stumbled upon her parents sharing a kiss in the small cupboard.

Daniel's car was already in the driveway when she arrived back at their cottage. He was in the kitchen, laptop open, frowning at the screen with the same expression she'd learned meant he was dealing with something unpleasant.

'It's good news,' she announced, setting down her bag with the happiest smile she'd had in weeks. 'Dad's fine. Medication interaction, not dementia. Dr Mitchell says he'll be back to normal within a fortnight.'

Daniel's face broke into a wide grin. 'That's wonderful news. You must be—' He stopped, studying her face more carefully. 'Are you alright? You look...'

'Like I might cry?' Amelia laughed, wiping at her eyes. 'Happy tears, I promise. I just... I was so scared, Daniel. I thought I was watching him disappear, and there was nothing I could do to stop it.'

'*Ma chérie*,' Daniel said softly, moving around the table to pull her into his arms. 'I'm so sorry you had to carry that fear alone.'

'I wasn't alone,' Amelia said against his chest, breathing in the familiar scent of his cologne. 'You were there. At dinner, after—you understood what I was feeling before I even understood it myself.'

She felt him tense slightly, and when she pulled back to look at his face, there was something troubled in his expression.

'What's wrong?'

'My company. My job. Our future.'

Amelia's stomach clenched. After the rollercoaster of emotions she'd experienced today, she wasn't sure she could handle bad news. 'Is this about Mrs Henderson?'

'Yes.'

Amelia sank into her usual chair at the kitchen table, bracing herself. 'All right. Tell me everything.'

'Mrs Henderson is very relieved that someone finally told her the complete truth about corporate intentions.' Daniel's smile was rueful. 'She's been asking increasingly pointed questions about the timeline. I think she suspected something wasn't quite right.'

'So what happens now?'

'I've told her Mrs Henderson the truth about why I was sent here and what the company wanted. I told her that if she thought it was ethical, as I have resigned from the company, I was happy to advise her. No charge.'

'And?'

'And then I told her that I hoped that the woman I love might consider building a life with someone who's finally learned the difference between career advancement and honesty.'

The word "love" hung in the air between them. Tears pricked at her eyes again—happy tears, complicated tears, tears for all the misunderstandings that had led them to this moment.

'I love you too,' she said simply, and watched relief flood his features. 'But Daniel, if we're going to do this—really do this—there can't be any more secrets. No more work issues taking precedence over personal honesty.'

'No more secrets,' Daniel promised. 'Though I should warn you, my family is going to have opinions about my career change.'

'Career change?'

'I can't stay in a job that requires me to treat people like strategic assets rather than human beings. I'm done with corporate acquisition work.'

Amelia reached across the table to take his hands. 'What will you do instead?'

'I was thinking about agricultural consulting. I have the qualifications, and I can see how well Guy and Oli are doing. I am sure there's a market for my skills.'

'In vineyards, you mean?'

'No. Helping farmers implement sustainable technologies rather than seeing them fail and sell out to big corporations. It will mean travel, probably irregular income at first, but it will be honest work. And I would like to base myself in Duckinwilla Creek.'

'Are you sure?"

'I've never been more certain of anything in my life.

'It sounds perfect.'

'Even if it means we might have to live on your teacher's salary for a while?'

'A kept man? I think I could handle that if it means you staying here,' Amelia said. 'We'll manage. Besides, Charlotte's been after me to help expand the guest accommodation side of *Maison de Rêve*. Between your agricultural expertise and my organisational skills, we could probably develop some sort of farm-stay consultancy.'

Daniel's eyes lit up. 'You've been thinking about this.'

'I've been thinking about a lot of things,' Amelia admitted. 'Including how to tell my family that I'm in love with a man who might not be staying in Australia.'

'About that...' Daniel squeezed her hands. 'How do you feel about having that conversation over dinner Friday night? I believe I've been invited to the family celebration.'

'Of course you have. But you want to tell my family about us at Dad's celebration dinner? About us? About the Henderson deal, about your job situation, about everything?'

'I want to stop living in fear of what people might think if they know the truth about me,' Daniel said. 'Starting with the people who matter most to you.'

***

Friday evening, the entire family—Lisette had come home for the weekend—assembled in *Grandmère* and Papa's grand dining room, but this time the atmosphere was entirely different.

Dad looked more like himself than he had in weeks, cracking jokes and finishing his sentences. Mum was glowing with relief, and even Guy seemed more relaxed than usual. Amelia grinned as she cracked a joke with Oli.

'So,' *Grandmère* said over the main course, fixing Daniel with her sharp blue gaze, 'Daniel asked me if he could share some news with the family. While everyone is here.'

Lisette caught Amelia's eye with her eyebrows raised, and Daniel smiled as Amelia shrugged.

'Actually, I have news to share,' he said. 'Several pieces of news, in fact.'

He told them about his work with Mrs Henderson, about the technology acquisition deal, about his company's expectations and his growing reservations about corporate agriculture practices. He explained how meeting Amelia had changed his perspective on what he wanted from life, and how he'd decided to leave the Langlois company to start his own agricultural consulting firm.

'And,' he said, reaching for Amelia's hand, 'I've asked Amelia to consider another partnership. A personal one.'

'Well,' Mum said finally. 'It's about time.'

Amelia nearly choked on her wine. 'Mum!'

'What? We've all been watching you two dance around each other for weeks. You've been so happy since Daniel moved in, and he looks at you like you're very special.' Ellen smiled at Daniel. 'Which you are, of course.'

'We all know better than that, Daniel,' Lisette teased. 'Wait until you live with Amelia a bit longer.'

'I quite agree that you have both been happy,' *Grandmère* said, raising her wine glass. 'Though I must say, young man, your poker face needs work. You've been broadcasting your feelings since that first morning I found you in the kitchen.'

'You knew?' Amelia stared at her grandmother.

'*Ma chérie*, I've been watching people fall in love for seventy-eight years. You develop a sense for these things.' *Grandmère*'s eyes twinkled with mischief. 'Besides, no man makes coffee for someone he considers merely a housemate.'

'The coffee was a dead giveaway,' Dad agreed solemnly. 'That and the way he started reading the agricultural section of the paper after you mentioned you were interested in sustainable farming.'

Daniel looked around the table with the expression of someone who'd just realised he'd been thoroughly transparent in his attempts at subtlety. 'Was I really that obvious?'

'Painfully so,' Oliver said cheerfully. 'But in a good way. We all love seeing Amelia happy. Looks like you've been successful where we all failed miserably.'

'And we like seeing her with someone who appreciates her properly,' Julien added. 'About time someone recognised what we've always known—our sister is extraordinary.'

Tears spilled over Amelia's cheeks, but again, they were entirely happy tears. Looking around the table at her family's faces—Dad, clear-eyed and following every word, Mum beaming with satisfaction, her siblings teasing and openly approving—the last of Amelia's fears about the future finally evaporated.

'So,' Charlotte said, clearly unable to

contain her excitement any longer. 'When's the wedding?'

'Charlotte!' Amelia protested, but she was laughing.

'What? I'm just saying, if you're going into business together, you might as well make it official. Besides, I've already started planning the reception menu in my head.'

'One thing at a time,' Daniel said diplomatically, but Amelia caught the look he gave her—full of promise and the love she'd never dared to dream of.

Later, as they drove home through the warm Queensland evening, Amelia sighed.

Daniel reached over and took her hand. 'You okay?'

'I am. What a week! Dad's health scare resolved, you've resigned, and my precious independence has turned into a partnership that feels like the beginning of everything I didn't know I wanted. Does that make sense?'

'It does. So, no regrets, my love?' Daniel asked, echoing his question from that first morning they'd woken up together.

'Not even close,' Amelia replied, squeezing his hand. 'Though I should probably warn you—my family's going to expect regular updates on our business venture. And Charlotte's going to start dropping wedding hints at every opportunity.'

'I can handle Charlotte's hints,' Daniel said with a smile. 'As for regular updates... I'm rather looking forward to having news worth sharing.'

As they pulled into the driveway—their driveway, Amelia thought with a thrill of happiness—she realised that everything she'd thought she wanted when she moved out of the family farm had been just the beginning. Independence had been important, but a partnership was going to be extraordinary.

'Daniel?' she said as they walked up the front path together.

'Hmm?'

'Thank you for staying. For fighting for this, for us, even when it would have been easier to just leave.'

'*Ma chérie*,' Daniel said, stopping to pull her into his arms under the jacaranda tree. 'Nothing about loving you has been easy. But it's been the best thing that's ever happened to me.'

As he kissed her under the star-filled Queensland sky, Amelia knew that whatever challenges lay ahead—building their business, working at the pre-school, navigating a relationship, and managing her family's inevitable wedding obsession—they would face them together.

And that made all the difference in the world.

Epilogue

Six months later

The morning of the wedding dawned bright and clear, which Amelia took as a good omen since the weather forecast had been predicting disaster for a week. She woke in her childhood bedroom at the farm—Charlotte had insisted on proper pre-wedding traditions—to the sound of what could only be described as organised chaos echoing through the house.

'Amélie!' *Grandmère*'s voice carried up the stairs with the confidence of a woman who'd been orchestrating family events for sixty years 'The flowers have arrived, and Charlotte has opinions about their arrangement!'

'Of course she does,' Amelia muttered, stretching luxuriously in bed. Through her window, she could see the marquee that had been set up in the back paddock, white and elegant against the green cane fields. By this evening, it would be filled with a mixture of Johnsons and Duponts, Australian farmers and French vintners, all celebrating the improbable instant love story that had started with a housing mix-up and ended with the most beautiful wedding Duckinwilla Creek had seen in years.

A knock on her door interrupted her thoughts. 'Come in!'

Lisette appeared in the doorway, already dressed in her bridesmaid dress and looking suspiciously triumphant. 'Good morning, bride-to-be. Ready for the most important day of your life?'

'Ready for breakfast,' Amelia replied. 'And coffee. Lots of coffee, please.'

'Already handled. Charlotte's made enough food to feed half of Queensland, and Daniel and his father dropped in with that French coffee machine his parents shipped over especially for today. *Grandmère* took it and shooed them back to the hotel.'

'How's Daniel holding up?'

'Like a man who's about to marry the love of his life and couldn't be happier about it,' Lisette said with a grin. 'Though Oliver may have traumatised him slightly with exaggerated explanations of traditional Australian wedding reception activities.'

'Oliver didn't actually—'

'No, but Daniel's expression when Oli mentioned the girl jumping out of the wedding cake was absolutely priceless. I may have taken photos.'

'Oli has come out of his shell since Sarah's been with him.' Amelia laughed, feeling the nervous excitement that had been building for weeks finally settle into simple joy. 'Is his family managing all right?'

'Daniel's parents are lovely, and they seem genuinely charmed by our family's particular brand of chaos. His mother spent an hour with Mum discussing sustainable farming practices, and his father's been helping Dad with the irrigation system repairs.' Lisette's expression grew more serious. 'They're good people, Amelia. And they clearly adore Daniel almost as much as they're going to adore you. What about the business? Are you both happy with the progress?'

'Henderson Vineyard Consulting is officially launched as of last week, complete with their first three client contracts and a waiting list that's apparently growing daily. Mrs Henderson couldn't be more pleased with how the licensing deal turned out, and she's already talking about expanding the educational programmes.' Amelia's warm glow of satisfaction grew as she told Lisette of the success of their business. The past six months had been a whirlwind of wedding planning, business development, and learning how to be partners in every sense of the word. There had been challenges—navigating the complexities of setting up the business, organising a visa, managing family expectations about wedding details, figuring out how to work together without driving each other completely bonkers— but they'd faced every obstacle together.

'Amelia!' Charlotte's voice joined the morning chorus of family members coordinating details. 'The hairdresser's here, and she wants to start with you first!'

'Coming!' Amelia called back, patted her hair that was now her natural strawberry blonde, and then turned to Lisette. 'How do I look?'

'Like someone who's about to make the smartest decision of her life,' Lisette replied softly. 'I'm proud of you, you know, Melie. For taking the risk, for choosing love over safety, for building something extraordinary with someone who deserves you.'

'Thanks, Lis. That means more than you know.'

The morning passed in a blur of hair appointments and makeup sessions, of photographs with various family combinations and last-minute adjustments to floral arrangements. Amelia was swept along in the efficient chaos of various family members who'd appointed themselves wedding coordinators, each with their tasks and strong opinions about proper implementation.

'The photographer wants family portraits in twenty minutes,' Emily announced, appearing in the doorway with a clipboard and the expression of someone managing a military parade. 'Julien's rounding up the male contingent, Charlotte's dealing with a minor catering crisis, and *Grandmère*'s giving the officiant detailed instructions about ceremony protocol.'

'What kind of catering crisis?' Amelia asked, slightly alarmed.

'Nothing catastrophic. Just Charlotte discovering that the caterers don't understand the difference between her *coq au vin* recipe and the simplified version they'd planned to prepare. She's currently conducting a cooking lesson in the marquee kitchen.'

Amelia grinned. 'Of course she is.'

By noon, the final preparations were complete, and Amelia was alone in her childhood bedroom, looking at her reflection in the full-length mirror Charlotte had dragged upstairs for the occasion. The dress was perfect—vintage lace with modern alterations, elegant yet understated. Her hair was styled in soft waves that caught the light, and the sapphire earrings *Grandmère* had lent her brought out the blue in her eyes.

She looked, she thought with surprise, like a bride. Not just someone dressed up for a formal occasion, but a woman about to make a very important promise to the man she loved. A soft knock interrupted her thoughts. 'Come in.'

Dad appeared in the doorway, looking handsome in his formal suit and a wide smile on his face.

'You look beautiful, sweetheart,' he said quietly. 'Your mother's crying already, and the ceremony doesn't start for another hour.'

'How are you feeling, Dad? Not too tired from all the chaos?'

'I'm feeling grateful,' Hugo replied, moving to stand beside her at the mirror. 'Grateful that you found someone who loves you the way you deserve to be loved. Grateful that my health scare turned out to be nothing serious. Grateful that you took the risk of moving out and building your own life, even when it scared all of us.'

'It scared me too,' Amelia admitted.

'The best decisions usually do.' Dad squeezed her hand gently. 'Are you ready to do this?'

Amelia thought about Daniel, probably getting similar encouragement from his own family in the hotel where he'd spent the night. She thought about their morning conversations over excellent coffee, about the business they were building together, about a future full of possibilities they'd chosen instead of the safe, predictable lives they could have settled for.

'I'm ready,' she said, and meant it completely.

The ceremony itself passed in a blur.

Walking down the aisle on Dad's arm, seeing Daniel's face light up when he saw her, the mix of tears and laughter as they exchanged the vows they'd written themselves. Charlotte's reading was perfect, Guy's coordination of the music was flawless, and *Grandmère*'s supervision ensured that every detail met her exacting standards.

But what Amelia would remember most clearly was the moment when Daniel took her hands and promised, in front of both their families, to choose her every day for the rest of their lives. To build something extraordinary together, to face whatever challenges came their way as partners, to never let fear make decisions for them again.

'I love you,' he said as they were pronounced husband and wife, 'and I'm going to spend the rest of my life proving worthy of this gift.'

'You already have,' Amelia replied, and kissed him while their combined families cheered.

The reception was everything Charlotte had promised and more—excellent food, dancing that went well into the night, and speeches that ranged from heartfelt to hilarious.

'So,' Oliver said during his best man speech, slightly tipsy on French champagne. 'When Daniel first showed up at our family dinner looking like he'd rather be anywhere else, I thought Amelia had finally lost her mind. But it turns out she just recognised something the rest of us took a while to see—that sometimes the best things happen when you're brave enough to share your life with someone worth the risk.'

As the evening wound down and guests began to drift away, Amelia and Daniel were alone on the dance floor, swaying to music perfect for the moment they were sharing.

'No regrets?' Daniel asked, echoing the question that had become their private joke.

'Not even close,' Amelia replied, looking around at the remnants of their perfect day— family members chatting, fairy lights twinkling in the Queensland darkness, the promise of their future stretching out before them like an invitation to adventure.

'Good,' Daniel said, pulling her closer. 'Because I have plans for us, Mrs Dupont.'

'Oh, do you now? And what sort of plans would those be?'

'The kind that involves excellent coffee every morning, terrible jokes at inappropriate moments, and building something extraordinary together for the next fifty years or so.'

'Sounds perfect,' Amelia said, and kissed her husband under the stars while their families cleaned up around them.

Some love stories, she thought drowsily as Daniel spun her around the empty dance floor, were worth every risk you had to take to find them.

And this one, she knew with absolute certainty, was going to be extraordinary.

All Together Now...
Coming in September

The afternoon sun streamed through the jacaranda tree as Amelia adjusted the trestle table for the third time, surveying the back garden of the cottage she and Daniel had called home for the past eight months. The space wasn't huge, but it had become the unofficial neutral ground for Johnson family gatherings—close enough to *Grandmère* and Papa's estate for easy access, far enough from the main farm to feel relaxed rather than formal.

'Stop fussing with the table,' Daniel said, emerging from the kitchen with a platter of marinated chicken. 'It's perfect, and besides, your family's more interested in the food than the presentation.'

'Says the man who spent twenty minutes arranging the salads in order of colour coordination,' Amelia replied, but she stepped back from the table with a smile. 'I just want everything to be nice. It feels like ages since we've all been together properly.'

'Two weeks,' Daniel corrected, firing up the

barbecue. 'It's been exactly two weeks since Charlotte's birthday dinner.'

'That was different. That was the formal dining room, best behaviour, *Grandmère* supervising everything. This is supposed to be relaxed family time.'

'You're nervous. Why are you nervous?'

Amelia shrugged, unable to articulate the vague unease that had been building all week. Mum had called to suggest the family barbecue with an unusual note of formality in her voice—not quite her casual "let's get everyone together" tone. Dad had been unusually quiet during their last visit, and even *Grandmère* had seemed more thoughtful than usual.

She was sure something was going on.

***

The Johnson family faces a double upheaval when Ellen and Hugo Johnson announce they're selling the farm to move to an over-55s coastal village, while *Grandmère* and Papa decide to enter a retirement home. With the future of both the family farm and the General Store uncertain, the entire Johnson clan must come together to make life-changing decisions in just two months.

Sometimes the biggest challenges bring out the best in families, and home is worth fighting for together.

Pre-order in print or eBook below.

Print:
https://annieseatonstore.ecwid.com/All-Together-Now-p765284790

eBook: https://books2read.com/u/4A6NJe

Also by Annie Seaton

Daughters of the Darling
From Across the Sea
Over the River
By the Billabong
Beneath Still Waters

A Bec Whitfield Mystery
Bowen River
Shadows on the Shore
Storm Season

Duckinwilla Days
Coming Home
Secrets and Surprises
Wishes and Whispers
Chasing Dreams
New Beginnings
All Together Now

The Enchanted Village series
A Magic Christmas

Home to the Outback
Lucy
Angie
Jemima

Isabella

Porter Sisters Series

Kakadu Sunset
Daintree
Diamond Sky
Hidden Valley
Larapinta
Kakadu Dawn

Others

Whitsunday Dawn
Undara
Osprey Reef
East of Alice
One Summer in Tuscany
Four Seasons Short and Sweet
Follow the Sun
Ten Days in Paradise
Deadly Secrets
Adventures in Time
Silver Valley Witch
The Emerald Necklace
A Clever Christmas
Christmas with the Boss
Her Christmas Star
The Emerald Necklace

The Augathella Girls Series

Outback Roads
Outback Sky
Outback Escape
Outback Wind
Outback Dawn
Outback Moonlight
Outback Dust
Outback Hope
Boxed Sets
Augathella Girls 1-4
Augathella Girls 5-8

Augathella Short and Sweet Series
An Augathella Surprise
An Augathella Baby
An Augathella Spring
An Augathella Christmas
An Augathella Wedding
An Augathella Easter
An Augathella Masquerade Ball
Boxed Set
Augathella Short and Sweet 1-3
Augathella Short and Sweet 1-4

Sunshine Coast Series
Waiting for Ana
The Trouble with Jack
Healing His Heart

Sunshine Coast Boxed Set

The Richards Brothers Series
The Trouble with Paradise
Marry in Haste
Outback Sunrise
Richards Brothers Boxed Set

Bondi Beach Love Series
Beach House
Beach Music
Beach Walk
Beach Dreams
The House on the Hill Boxed Set

Second Chance Bay Series
Her Outback Playboy
Her Outback Protector
Her Outback Haven
Her Outback Paradise
Boxed Set
The McDougalls of Second Chance Bay Set

Love Across Time Series
Come Back to Me
Follow Me
Finding Home
The Threads that Bind

Boxed Set
Love Across Time 1-4

Bindarra Creek Books
Worth the Wait
Full Circle
Secrets of River Cottage
A Clever Christmas
A Place to Belong
Hearts in Harmony

Awards

2025: Finalist- Romantic Suspense category - RUBY award-*From Across the Sea*

2023: Winner - Long contemporary novel category, RUBY award -*Larapinta.*

2023: Finalist - Australian Romance Readers Awards- *Kakadu Dawn,* the sixth and final book in the Porter Sisters series.

2018 and 2020: Finalist - for the NZ KORU Award.

2017: Winner - Best Established Author of the Year 2017 AUSROM

2017: Winner - Author of the Year, 2014 AUSROM

 Best Established Author, AUSROM Readers' Choice.

2016, 2017, 2018, 2019: Longlisted - Sisters in Crime Davitt Awards

2016: Finalist - Book of the Year, Long Romance, RWA Ruby Awards for *Kakadu Sunset*

2015: Winner - Best Established Author of the Year AUSROM

About the Author

Annie Seaton lives near the beach on the mid-north coast of New South Wales. Her career and studies spanned the education sector, including working as an academic research librarian, a high-school principal and a university tutor until she took early retirement and fulfilled her lifelong dream of a full-time writing career.

Each winter, Annie and her husband leave the beach to roam the remote areas of Australia for story ideas and research. She is passionate about preserving the beauty of the Australian landscape and respecting the traditional ownership of the land. For those readers who cannot experience this journey personally, Annie seeks to portray the natural beauty of the Australian environment—its spiritual locations, stunning landscapes and unique wildlife.

Readers can contact Annie through her website, annieseaton.net, or find her on Facebook and Instagram.

www.ingramcontent.com/pod-product-compliance
Lightning Source LLC
Chambersburg PA
CBHW060604190726

48283CB00003B/1149